Becoming Home

FOSTER'S WAY
BOOK ONE

Margaret McGaffey Fisk

TTO
PUBLISHING

Cover created by Margaret McGaffey Fisk

TTO Publishing logo design by Blue Harvest Creative
www.blueharvestcreative.com

Becoming Home

Published by
TTO Publishing

ISBN-10: 1-63139-025-2
ISBN-13: 978-1-63139-025-8

First Print Edition

Visit the author at:

Website: margaretmcgaffeyfisk.com
Twitter: @Marfisk
Google Plus: +MargaretMcGaffeyFiskAuthor
Facebook: MargaretMcGaffeyFisk

Other Works by
Margaret McGaffey Fisk

UNCOMMON LORDS AND LADIES
(SWEET REGENCY ROMANCES)

Beneath the Mask
A Country Masquerade
An Innocent Secret

THE STEAMSHIP CHRONICLES
(STEAMPUNK ADVENTURE)

Safe Haven
Secrets
Threats
Gifts
Life and Law
Steam and Shadows

SEEDS AMONG THE STARS
(SCIENCE FICTION ADVENTURE)

Shafter
Trainee
The Captain's Chair (Indie Traders short story)
Apprentice

SHORT STORIES (eBook only)

When the Shoe Won't Fit
Forged
War Child
Curve of Her Claw (illustrated by Star Olsen)

Visit margaretmcgaffeyfisk.com for more information about these and other titles.

Chapter 1

The bright summer sun cast shadows across Main Street as Celia Baker strolled toward her small cottage home at the end of a long day at the bookstore. She brushed at a patch of cardboard shavings on her skirt. Good, clean dust. A breeze puffed out the fabric and she clamped her skirt down with both hands, laughing along with the rush of air. She enjoyed all the natural sounds she could hear without the constant blare of traffic and voices bouncing from tall buildings. Even more, she didn't need to clutch her purse whenever she left the house.

Celia stretched both hands above her head and fought the need to spin in a circle, knowing the neighboring shopkeepers would see her and actually notice.

A car engine came to life. Its rumble shattered the peace, so different from the city where one more engine made no impact. Then the bells of the church three blocks away rang four o'clock. Celia paused to listen to the deep-throated tones before realizing she'd stayed after her shift to talk to Melanie for much too long. If she didn't hurry, she'd miss the chance of something wonderful at Peterson's Buy-Sell-Trade store.

A frown pinched her forehead, and she drew in a deep breath, forcing bad memories away, but she couldn't stop the hand rubbing the center of her chest.

Three months ago, she'd been deep in exhaust and the kind of grime that no amount of scrubbing could remove. Celia only needed to close her eyes to see the children, runaways or those removed from home by the state. They were always desperate, always needy, and never willing to accept help.

Her heart accelerated despite attempts to massage away the strain. The beat pounded in her ears, and she listened for the hiccup. For all she hated leaving the city kids to fend for themselves, this warning had sent her from a busy life of helping them through the tangles of bureaucracy and bad foster homes to the small town of Foster's Way.

She needed the town more than she wanted to admit. Its name held multiple meanings for her: a way out of the desolation, a way to recover her life, a place to rediscover who she could be if she didn't have to fear for her safety at the grocery store, and a place where people actually cared for their children.

Celia smiled though she didn't feel it yet, determined to make the most of this new chance without weighing it down with her past. What did it matter if the highlight of her day was an extra half-hour of chitchat with her twenty-two-year-old coworker or the search for exotic items in a pawnshop? She was happy here. If she felt restless, it was only because she still needed to settle in. Maybe the path to greater purpose didn't line the pocketed asphalt, but neither did the road to an early grave.

Mrs. Michaels waved to her from the bakery as she passed. Celia waved back, her smile softening. The people here were proof enough a better world existed outside the city. She needed that world, had needed it her whole life only she'd been too blind to know it.

Mr. Peterson came out to sweep his front step as she neared the shop, his wild gray hair tossed about his head as if he'd been in the wind, not her.

"Anything interesting today?" she asked in a ritual they'd created soon after she'd taken the job at the bookstore down the street.

He laughed. "Always something, Miss Baker, always something. I put the newest in the window just this afternoon. Go ahead and take a peek."

She hadn't waited for his invitation.

Her reflection looked pale and a bit pinched, but Mr. Peterson had been too nice to mention it. She smoothed her light brown hair into place after the wind's games, and leaned against the window.

"You'll put smudges on the glass just like the Academy boys," Mr. Peterson complained.

Celia ignored him as she always did except for the first time shortly after she'd moved here in the spring. He'd been so shocked and embarrassed when she'd jerked away and cleaned the window with her sweater he hadn't said a word for three days, but they'd grown used to each other since.

He hummed a song under his breath, too low for her to identify, and Celia turned her attention to the items in the front displays. She never found a magic lamp that could solve her slight discontent, or fix her weak heart, but she didn't really expect one.

"Any lamps?" she asked, the silly thought reminding her she couldn't read in her new favorite chair, one she'd found here last week, because the overhead didn't shine bright enough in the corner. "I'd be interested in a reading light."

Mr. Peterson shrugged. "You'll have to look. There's a desk lamp on the other side, but I'd guess you're talking about something a little taller to go with that armchair." Mr. Peterson had roped some of the Academy High School kids into moving it for her, something unheard of where she'd come from.

Celia grinned and pushed the bangs off her face in what had rapidly become a habit. "What would I do without this place?" she asked. You've almost furnished my whole house."

He frowned and shook his head. "Isn't right for a young woman to have nothing of her own. Didn't you live somewhere in that city you came from? And what about your family? Where's your ugly old chair from an Aunt Fran?"

She tapped him on the shoulder as she passed him to get to the other side. "Nothing worth keeping from there." Though she said the words lightly, the truth of them weighed her down.

Celia had taken nothing much from her family when she ran away at twelve. She'd been lucky to survive. Having a place, owning things, had never been important before.

She glanced at the window, lost in thoughts of her past, only to freeze. A sigh whispered from her lips as she stared at the burnished wood of a well-loved guitar.

"I've always wanted to play," she said, the words escaping without conscious thought.

"You should be careful, Miss Baker. A shopkeeper could take advantage of a statement like that."

Celia turned to Mr. Peterson and laughed. "A disreputable shopkeeper maybe. Not you."

"Well, come on in then and we'll see what we can do. A boy brought the guitar in. I didn't want to take it, but he had a birthday card proving the gift was his own. I only took it on commission, figuring his mom or dad would show up and reclaim it." The old man shrugged. "Guess he had the right of it, though. I held the guitar in the back for a full week with no inquiries."

Celia's eyes narrowed, old instincts rising to the surface.

"How did he look?" she asked. "Hungry? And his clothes?"

"Miss Baker, this isn't like where you came from." Mr. Peterson gave her shoulder a gentle pat. "He looked just fine. Healthy and well dressed. If he needs the money, it isn't for food or drugs, not around here."

She stared at him for a moment, then laughed, pushing her worries away. No, Foster's Way wasn't like her old home. It wasn't perfect, no matter what Mr. Peterson wanted to believe. But neither were there runaways begging for handouts on every street or kids trapped in a system that drove them to dangerous occupations. Just because she'd lived where every child had been at risk before didn't mean she should go looking for them here.

Especially not with the doctor's warning. A coworker had forced her to get an appointment, never guessing it would end Celia's old life altogether.

"You're right. And I'm retired."

"Miss Baker, you're much too young to be retiring from anything." He tucked the broom in its corner and placed both hands on the counter to level his best stare in her direction. "What you need is a man in your life to remind you it's not all doom and gloom. When you told me what you did in the city, I couldn't believe a pretty young thing like you would be mixed up with crime and drugs and all."

This time Celia's laugh came out full and robust. "Why Mr. Peterson, I do believe you're a little too old for me," she said in her best imitation of a Southern belle.

He caught her hand and pressed a dry kiss to the back, the contrast in their skin tone making her look all too fragile. "I fear you're right, Miss Baker, but if I could turn back the clock…"

She tugged her hand away with a smile. "Could you turn it back to the point where you were going to sell me the guitar?"

"Of course I can. Let me get it out of the window. I'm no player myself, but it sure had a sweet tone when I tried. I've even got one of those how-to books around here somewhere if you'd like me to find it."

"Thanks," Celia said, her fingers itching to touch the strings. She just needed a hobby, something to fill those lonely hours, especially with the weekend stretching before her. She'd never had quiet hours before. And she certainly didn't need a boyfriend no matter what Mr. Peterson believed. She'd seen how men treat their women often enough, even the good ones, and she didn't need that kind of complication.

BRIAN LAKES TORE THE SKIN on his third finger of the day and cursed under his breath. The wallpaper knife fell to the floor, whispering against the few strips he'd managed to remove. Brian stared at the section of wall he'd planned to clear today and wished for the feel of steel strings beneath his fingertips instead. Those calluses did him no good in this task.

"Nick, can you bring me a soda?" Brian called to his son. He used a sweat-stained bandana to wipe his forehead then stretched both hands over his head, listening to the crackle and pop of his spine while he waited.

"Nick?" he called again after a moment of silence.

His son came from deeper in the house, feet dragging and sandy blond head sunk on his shoulders.

Brian held back a sigh. "Why don't you get one for yourself, too, then come here and help."

"Whatever."

Even Nick's sour attitude made Brian's heart clench with lost moments.

He watched his son vanish, wishing he could have been there more, to have seen Nick grow from a baby to the twelve-year-old before him. Brian wiped at his face again, swearing the move was reflex and had nothing to do with the moisture gathering in his eyes.

Nick had it rough.

Brian wished he hadn't made it harder, but he couldn't stay in Nick's house. He couldn't live where Kaitlin's fear and hatred had torn them apart.

"Here."

While he'd sat there staring into space, Nick had already returned with a cola—one bottle.

"You didn't want one?" Brian asked, trying to keep his voice steady.

"No."

Nick stayed there, but only because Brian had made it a requirement in one of their early clashes. He wouldn't volunteer any information, and he wouldn't offer to help, but he would stand there because Brian said he had to.

This time Brian's sigh refused to be suppressed.

"Go on back to whatever you were doing," he told his son, the exhalation of air still heavy between them.

The boy started walking in a smooth motion as if he'd never had to stop at all.

It seemed as though Brian was always watching Nick disappear. He wished he could do something to connect with his son, to bring them past the years Kaitlin had kept them apart. He'd thought restoring this rambling Victorian would give them shared experiences, but for that to work, Nick had to be involved.

Brian lifted the knife to the wall once more and shoved. The wallpaper split with the force of his push, but so did the plaster behind it, sending up a cloud of dust.

He coughed hard and slugged a gulp of cola, but the carbonation only made him cough harder. He glared at the latest divot to join a growing number and wanted to throw it all away. The house, this town, even his belated attempt at parenthood.

Brian pushed to his feet and crossed the room, the glass bottle still in his hand. Curtains. They had to get curtains, something not too frilly for two men on their own, but cloth to make this house more of a home and less of a naked, abandoned building.

He'd seen the neighbors peering in his windows, curious. They'd smiled and waved when he caught them at it. All except the old lady in the house to the left.

Brian shook his head and laughed. Every neighborhood had its gossip. He'd lucked out in choosing a house right next door.

He looked out the bare window onto a street much like the one where he'd grown up, even if the town itself wasn't.

Small roads, houses spaced so you didn't look out into your neighbor's bedroom, and good-sized yards. A calm, peaceful place with none of the frantic energy of Nick's—and his—hometown. Foster's Way had seemed like the perfect place to heal and reconnect when he'd researched relocation, and nothing would change his mind. Nick just needed time.

The echo of a line about lonely hearts and friendly neighbors teased him. His free hand curled around an invisible fretboard, but Brian forced his fingers to straighten and pushed the thought away.

He was a responsible father now. He might have screwed up his marriage with all the time on the road, but he wouldn't screw up Nick's life. The boy had no one since his mother and stepfather died in an accident, no one but a father he barely remembered.

If Brian had one thing to do over, he would never have let Kaitlin's bitterness keep him from his son.

His mouth twisted into a humorless smile.

Maybe someday he'd hold to that vow. Even dead, she still pushed him around, pushed him away from his hometown.

If he'd been able to force down the memories, the bitter fragments of his past, maybe Nick wouldn't be so withdrawn. Brian had taken him from his friends, from everything his son had known, all because he couldn't handle the haunting.

Moving had seemed like a good idea when he'd come up with it. A new start for both of them, away from the taint of Kaitlin's death—and life—in a place where they could just be average folks, a place to begin again without the weight of past mistakes.

Brian let out a sour laugh.

If he wanted to, he could get a whole new album out of his own misery. No looking for material. He embodied the country music spirit.

My girl done torn my heart out and left me for dead with an infant in my arms.

Except Nick wasn't an infant, and Brian wasn't the one who'd passed on.

He lowered the now-empty soda bottle to the windowsill and left it there, knowing he'd been only seconds away from chucking it through the window. He could afford to replace the glass, but he didn't want the reputation that kind of behavior would bring about, or the questions it might raise.

No, he just needed to keep his hands busy and his mind on figuring Nick out. He'd bought the neglected house so he'd have something to keep him sane, but he'd imagined the two of them bringing it to life, restoring it, together.

It had been a pretty dream.

The section of wall called to him. It would never get done if he didn't put knife to paper. Nick would come around. He just needed time to grieve, time to realize this stranger was a permanent part of his life now. Nick needed to accept his father wouldn't up and disappear no matter what.

Chapter 2

Bang. Bang.

Celia jerked awake, her whole body tense.

Shouts followed the gunshots, young voices.

She pulled the blanket against her light cotton nightdress and tried not to tremble.

Where was her cell phone? Should she go investigate first before calling the police? Did a kid out there need her help?

A child's voice, high enough that its owner could not have passed puberty, cut through the moment of silence.

Before Celia could put together a conscious thought, she'd leapt from the bed, run across the room, and started jamming one leg after another into her slacks. Shoes next, no time for socks. The rough canvas scraped her bare feet, but the discomfort had no importance.

Her hand closed around the metal doorknob, or rather around the hand-knit doorknob cover her next-door neighbor had given her for a house-warming present, and memory returned.

She dragged in a deep breath, listening for her racing heart to settle into a more normal rhythm. Only then did she laugh at herself.

High crime in the sleepy streets of Foster's Way. The police were lucky to bust some teens smoking out behind the high school in any given year. She knew. She'd asked before moving here.

Celia slipped out of the uncomfortable shoes and danced against the cool hardwood floor until her feet adjusted. The cottage had good insulation. Cool in the summer and warm in the winter, though she'd yet to test the last.

She crossed her bedroom and tugged open the thick curtains. Bright sunlight flooded in, wiping away the last of her uneasiness.

The scene outside in no way resembled the smog-filled, crowded intensity of the city she'd left behind. The kids here didn't flinch away from their parents, and she'd never seen a parent cuff a kid since arriving. Discipline, sure, but not the casual violence that had taken the place of love among the kids she worked with.

The padded bench below the window called to her, and Celia curled up on it so she could rest her elbows on the windowsill and watch the kids play.

Bang.

She flinched, then laughed as cries of, "I'll get you, you thief," burst through the morning air.

Cops and robbers had a different feel when sirens could mean your one stable parent, or favorite brother, vanished behind bars or into the ground. It meant being swept up and put into another foster home with seven other kids. She'd never had the chance to play like these kids. She'd never been safe enough.

A wistful smile tugged at her cheek, and she wondered what the kids would say if she donned a blue shirt and went out to join them. They seemed to like her well enough. All her neighbors seemed like nice people. She'd never felt so welcome.

The curtain slipped from her fingers, plunging the room in darkness again.

More likely they'd just laugh at her, even if not in a mean way. She could live with being an eccentric, but she couldn't recapture a childhood she'd never had.

Still, a smile stayed on her lips as she went through her morning routine. If nothing else, the abrupt awakening reminded her why she'd chosen this place. It told her she could be happy here.

THE STENCH OF FRESH PAINT filled Brian's nostrils despite the shower he'd just taken. It was still early for dinner, but he couldn't face another paintbrush or paint can.

He leaned out the window of his bedroom and searched their backyard for any sign of Nick. There was none.

The boy had refused to help with the remodeling again. He just stayed in his room and fed batteries to the handheld game machine his mother had given him last Christmas.

Brian didn't have the heart to take it away. No matter what his own feelings toward Kaitlin were, she'd been a good mom to their son. She'd set a standard he'd never be able to live up to. If Nick would even let him try.

They shared meals, Brian had mandated that much, but they didn't talk; they didn't connect.

He sighed and turned away to pull on a fresh pair of jeans and a new t-shirt. The smell of paint lingered in the house, but he'd almost finished one room. He could feel happy with the fact. If only he had more to be proud of.

His fingers twitched, curving into a familiar position he hoped they'd forget for a while at least. "I wouldn't give it up for you, Kaitlin, but Nick's mine now," he told her ghost. Sometimes only her looming presence kept him on the path he'd decided to follow.

He couldn't be a father if he was always on the road. Brian had few illusions. He was good, good enough so playing in some coffee house or bar would never suffice. Good enough he'd be "discovered" all over again and the road would call. The only way to make this work was to give it up.

He pushed a strand of black hair off his face and grimaced. His hair had grown too long in front, in back, and on the sides. Another month or two, and he'd look like a street bum if he didn't already. It had been years since he'd had to worry about mundane details.

What had given him the idea he could handle a devastated boy?

The question stung, but he didn't let it linger any more this time than he ever had. He marched out of the room and down the stairs, using the newel post to swing onto Nick's landing. When his son had chosen a different floor, Brian thought maybe the privacy would do Nick some good. Now, he wasn't so sure, but it was too late to change.

He wasn't sure of anything anymore.

"Hey, Nick," Brian said, poking his head through the open doorway. "You want to go in the backyard and throw a ball around? We could go down to the park, if you'd like."

Nick shuffled on the bed, but didn't even look up from the machine in his hand.

"Come on. You've been locked up in here all day. The fresh air will serve us both some good."

Nick curled his shoulders and focused more intently.

Brian marched into the room and put a hand on Nick's shoulder, forcing him to look up. "When I'm talking to you, I want to see your face," he said, trying hard to keep his tone level. "Now I asked you a question."

Nick shrugged off the touch and mumbled, "Mom said you couldn't throw straight if your life depended on it."

Brian surged away, fists clenched at his sides. Even if he'd been able to ignore her ghost, she kept harping at him after death…in Nick's voice. He sucked in a deep breath and blew it out slowly, trying to remember what the grief counselor had told him about the process.

She'd said he would have to handle attacks gently. Nick needed someone to blame for the accident, and he'd prove a convenient target.

He'd been so confident then, sure they'd connect as easily as they had when Nick was a baby. Brian might not have been around much, but when he was, they'd had fun. Hadn't they?

"How about I show you some chords on your guitar?" The offer slipped out before Brian thought it through, but why not. There was one thing he knew he was good at. Maybe he should stop pretending to be something he wasn't and work with his strengths.

"Your mom was right. I can't throw worth a darn," he added with a shaky laugh, trying to reach out to the boy.

Nick seemed to shrink into himself even more.

The residual anger Brian had fought off melted away entirely.

"Hey," he said, sitting down on the bed next to Nick. "How about it? I know you don't remember me from before, and your life has been nothing but a mess since I came back. But I'm trying, I really am. All this time, I've loved you even when..."

He choked on the words. True or not, it would do him no good to blame Nick's dead mother for keeping them apart.

Brian pushed to his feet and scanned the bedroom.

"Where are you keeping her? A guitar should never sit idle for too long or the strings go sour." He laughed. "Like a neglected girlfriend, though I suppose you're too young to know about that yet." He glanced at Nick, wondering if he'd accidentally discovered the problem. Had he separated a pair of lovers?

A blush colored Nick's neck and face before creeping up to his ears.

"I guess not. Maybe sour like a bottle of the milk you down in such great quantities."

"You don't drink an instrument," Nick mumbled, staring down at the game again.

Brian fought the need to snatch the game from Nick's hands, to throw the little machine across the room. Instead, he crouched on the floor and put a hand on Nick's arm.

"What about it then? She has a sweet voice. My first acoustic. Maybe you'll find you inherited something more from me than just my dashing features."

Nick shot him an incredulous look, and Brian sighed. Back when times were good, the phrase had been a joke between him and Kaitlin.

Nick was the image of Brian's ex-wife, petite to Brian's lanky and sandy blond to his black hair. But Nick had been too young to remember the teasing, to remember any happiness between his parents.

Brian almost gave up. He'd already pushed. What else could he do?

The stubborn streak that had served him well in the early years of proving himself on the music scene rose. He pushed to his feet, unwilling to walk away.

"Tell you what. I'll play the guitar while you play your game. If you get bored, maybe you'll let me show you a thing or two."

The thought of having a fretboard beneath his fingers distracted him for a moment, then he glanced up. Nick had shifted further onto the bed, further away from him.

Brian swallowed a sigh.

"Is she in the closet?" he asked, moving toward a door no different from the one opening onto this room. "I can tune her for you."

"It's not here."

"Oh, is she under your bed?"

"It's not here!"

The second time Brian heard what Nick had really said, but he still didn't understand it. "What do you mean 'not here'?"

Nick flinched as though he expected to be hit.

An icy chill poured over Brian.

He dropped to his knees, ignoring the ache as hard wood met hard bone. "You know I'd never hit you, Nick. Just tell me what you mean."

Nick stared down at his hands, and for a heartbeat, Brian thought his son had gone back to playing. But when he looked, the little machine lay discarded on the blanket, and Nick's fingers twisted together.

"Where's my guitar?" Brian asked again, stifling his anger as best he could.

Nick shoved off the end of the bed and crossed the room to his desk. The boy stood there, holding onto the back of his chair with enough force to whiten knuckles.

"It's not your guitar. You gave it to me. That makes it mine. I can do whatever I want with it."

Brian's eyes slid closed, and he saw image after image of the guitar smashed beyond recovery. Had Nick taken his anger out on the instrument?

He pushed the hair out of his face and stared at the floor. How would he ever understand a kid who could do something so destructive to something he loved?

"Where is she?" The words whispered out, and Brian realized he'd already begun planning a funeral. He could bury the pieces under the oak tree they had in the yard.

"I sold it."

The quiet statement brought Brian's head up to stare at his son, stunned.

"Why?" he choked out.

Nick started pacing, his matchstick arms swinging out on either side. "It's obvious we don't have enough money. We're living in a dump, and we never go out at all. Mom said you were rich. She said you were some kind of a hot shot. I've seen your picture in magazines before. I never thought you'd need my help."

Brian rocked onto his heels and stared at the boy who was his son, rewriting everything he'd believed he knew.

All this time while he'd seen Nick moping, his son had been working out a way to help with the expenses. Suddenly, the gulf between them didn't seem as far as he'd thought.

A laugh burst out of him and then another. Nick offered a shaky smile and Brian stood. He opened his arms wide, and for once, Nick took him up on it.

"Oh, Nick. I have got to learn to talk to you. I thought you understood all this." He waved at the room and the house beyond. "And I've been trying to keep things healthy, trying to do what your mother did."

Nick leaned back and looked him in the eye.

"You don't have to be Mom," he said with a wisdom Brian would never have expected. "You can't anyway."

Brian knelt down to meet his son's gaze straight on. "Tell you what. We'll go talk to whomever you sold the guitar to, buy her again, and go out for pizza. How does that sound?"

"You think we can? Get it back, I mean?" Nick's expression held a mix of hope and worry.

"Of course we can. They shouldn't have bought it from you in the first place."

"I showed him the card. It was mine, and I could prove it. Otherwise the guy wouldn't have bought it from me. I just wanted to help."

Brian gave Nick a quick hug and stood up. "Sure you did. But next time, talk to me first? We've sat at the same table so many times, but I don't think we've ever really talked."

"I'll try," Nick said, his voice soft.

Then he slipped his hand into Brian's, a gesture Brian would have thought the boy had outgrown years ago. The touch reassured Brian as well as his son. They had a long way to go, but at least now they were on the same road.

Chapter 3

Have you finished stocking the travel books?"

Celia glanced up from the new box she'd just opened and smiled at Melanie. "All done. I thought I'd get a start on the magazines."

Her coworker stepped through the curtain separating the work area from the main store and slapped a hand over the box, holding it closed. "Leave it. Your shift's almost over. Don't you have something else to do?"

Shifting her weight onto both heels, Celia met the calm stare of Melanie's blue eyes and wished she could say yes.

"I know that look. You're going home to sit there alone again aren't you? You never go anywhere. I know Foster's Way is tame compared to what you're used to, but we have a couple of bars and coffee houses where they do music at night. Rock, country and western, even jazz once. What's your pleasure?"

Celia laughed. "I get music all day here. Why would I go to some crowded place with so much noise?"

Melanie shook her blond curls. "Someday you're going to agree, and I'll just faint from surprise. But for now, your time's up. Go take your focus elsewhere. Remember what I said, though. You need to get out and see the town. Learn what we have to offer before you become some hermit, and everyone shakes their heads when you walk by."

Her knees ached when Celia pushed to her feet, but she enjoyed sorting out the new books. It was like touching different worlds.

"As if I can become a hermit with you hanging around. No one would believe me."

The younger woman's full-bodied laugh followed Celia as she went to pick up her coat and purse. Despite her refusal, the idea of music appealed—music, not the noise and crowds of some bar. Celia still felt too jumpy. She liked her peace and quiet.

The bell chimed as she left, reminding Celia of the call to music. When she'd been five years old, her mother gave her a jewelry box for Christmas. She'd kept her treasures in it, but most of the time she just wound the knob to listen to the tinkling sounds. It had been one of the few things she regretted leaving behind seven years later. She just couldn't stay in the same house with her stepfather any longer.

Celia reached Peterson's Buy-Sell-Trade and waved to the shopkeeper.

"Hello, Miss Baker. You coming in today?" He propped his broom against the wall and stepped down so they were almost level.

"Well, that depends. Have you got anything new to show me?" Something shifted inside her even as she teased the old man. She didn't want to look at new things.

"Actually," Celia added, putting up a finger to forestall his response, "I think I'm going to head on home. I've got a guitar to learn."

He tipped his hand as if he were wearing a hat and gave her a smile. "You do that. I'm surprised you aren't performing down at the coffee house by now. They have an open mic night, don't you know?"

Celia laughed aloud. "Hmm. I'll be staying far away from there with my guitar, I think. I haven't even opened the lesson book yet. No reason to torture anyone."

"Then you get right on it. I expect you'll be serenading me soon enough, but you need to practice first."

"That'll be the day." She laughed, thinking how long it would take her to get decent enough to play a song. Forever seemed nearer.

Mr. Peterson's face sunk into a frown, his jaw a mass of wrinkles. "I'm just not good enough for you then?" he asked, the twinkle in his eyes giving him away.

"Tell you what. I'll play for you just as soon as it won't make all the dogs in the neighborhood start howling. I like the peace of this place and won't be the one to break it."

He laughed with her and snagged the broom from the wall. "You do that, Miss Baker. You do that."

Her steps lighter, she almost skipped the rest of the way. She would try out the guitar. Even if she was awful at it, there was no one to hear.

As long as she kept her windows shut.

"It's down this way," Nick called, dancing ahead then running back for what must have been the millionth time. "Come on."

Brian shook his head as he stretched his legs into a faster stride. He was more out of shape than he'd thought, and a stitch made his side ache. Too many late nights up drinking before he'd collected Nick. All the renovation work he'd been doing might be time-consuming and exhausting, but it wasn't worth much exercise.

"You sure are slow."

Nick appeared at his side again, staring up at him.

"Yeah, well, I'm a few years older than you are." Brian stopped to stretch and noticed an old woman sitting on her porch.

"Hello," he called, trying to be neighborly.

She stared at him for a long, silent moment, then got up and walked into her house, the door slamming behind her.

Brian stood there, stunned.

What was her problem? It's not like he'd demanded anything of her.

He shook his head, surprised at the cold reaction, and long, black strands lashed around his face. He shoved the nearest hair behind his ears and laughed.

"I must look like some drugged-out hippie to these people."

"What's a hippie?" Nick asked, once again next to him.

What did other parents do with these questions?

Luckily, Nick lost interest and ran ahead again before Brian had to come up with an answer. He noticed his son had not asked about the drug part, but remembered hearing on the news about elementary schools and the anti-drug program. Why hadn't they taught Nick about hippies? Or was that a high school level course?

The sheer amount of information he needed and didn't know overwhelmed him. How could he have any idea what to do for Nick? Where did parents learn about this? Or did they let the school teach all the difficult stuff? He still needed to make sure the school accepted Nick's registration for the next term.

His gaze fell on his son, who was acting like a normal young boy or at least what Brian thought was normal, and smiled. It didn't matter if he had no experience. He'd figure it all out somehow. At least he had his son.

The next turn took them out of the residential area and on to Main Street. Small shops dotted its length, but Brian had only visited the grocery and hardware stores down at the other end. He'd been too busy, too focused on the house, to take the time to stroll around.

But Nick had obviously walked here and back often enough to know where this pawnshop was. Maybe Brian should be focusing more on learning about their new home than working on the house.

"There's a toy store, and a pet store, and a book store..."

Nick danced from foot to foot in front of Brian, sharing his knowledge freely.

Brian put a hand on Nick's shoulder to catch hold for just a moment. "Have you met any other kids? Do you play with anyone?"

At first it had just been a question, but when the words crossed his lips, Brian suddenly worried about the crowd Nick was hanging out with. He hadn't noticed his son leaving the house, but Nick had obviously spent some time running around.

A headshake with chin almost on chest was his answer. "No kids yet," Nick mumbled.

Relief flooded Brian, then congealed as he thought about what that meant. He crouched in front of his son and looked him right in the eye. "Just wait 'til school starts. You'll meet some kids there. It'll be okay. And until then you still have me, right?"

Nick's mouth tightened.

"Right?" Brian asked again, seeing their connection fading already.

Nick looked up at him for a long pause, then nodded. "Right."

Brian rewarded his son with a broad grin. "Let's go get the guitar."

Again, Nick curled his fingers around Brian's and tugged him forward.

A glance ahead quickened Brian's step with an instinct he hadn't felt in a long while. Something about the woman he saw two blocks further on caught his attention. He stood straighter despite the stitch in his side and started composing what he would say to her before he realized what he was doing.

Brian shook his head. He was a father now. He had no business chasing after women.

He slowed his pace, torn between laughter and anger. He hadn't played around when he and Kaitlin were together despite what she'd believed, but he was no saint. If not for Nick, he'd probably jog the distance separating him from the woman and at least find out why he found her compelling.

Instead, he let the breath whistle out between his teeth and watched her until she turned a corner a few blocks beyond. Something about her walk drew him, a stride that would make her at home anywhere. He could see her in downtown Nashville, even New York City, and no one would give her any trouble.

"Aren't you coming in? We're here."

Brian glanced toward the shop and read the sign even as he took in the jumble of items in the window.

"Buy, Sell, Trade," he murmured. "Looks like a pawnshop to me."

An older gentleman came out, his dark, wrinkled face split by a wide grin. "Been too many movies about pawnshops, son. People see those words on the sign, they'll think the mafia or money sharks have come to town. Me, I just take what people no longer want and find homes for the goods where they'll be appreciated."

He wiped his dusty hands on an apron that might once have been white and squinted at Nick. "Don't I know you?" He didn't pause long enough for Nick to answer before saying, "Of course I do. You're the boy with the guitar."

Brian stepped forward, trying to cut between the two though Nick shouldn't have been in any danger.

The shopkeeper nodded. "You're his father. Smart to tag along when picking up his money. Even here not everyone is trustworthy."

Before Brian could open his mouth to explain, the man turned and went through the door. "You all coming?" came floating back.

"Yeah, we're coming," Nick answered, tugging on Brian's arm.

It took a moment, though, for Brian to get moving.

He finally understood the man's meaning. They were too late. If the shopkeeper had money for Nick, he'd sold the guitar. Brian's eyes slipped closed, grief washing over him. He'd loved that guitar, had always planned for Nick to have it even when Kaitlin kept them apart. But maybe he'd rushed things, gave it away before his son could understand the significance.

Another tug and Brian started forward, at first numb, but then with a growing determination.

They reached the counter where the man was already pulling out an old metal cash box.

"Hold on. We don't want the money," Brian said, his hand pressing the box lid shut. "We need the guitar back."

The old man shook his head. "Now, I don't think that's possible. The buyer, well, she's mighty happy with it. And the boy showed me proof of ownership, such as it was. Unless he stole it somehow."

A tiny gasp escaped from Nick. Even if Brian had thought to use the excuse, he knew he couldn't. He'd given his son the guitar, and the giver had no say over what happened to the gift.

"Just write down her address for me, and I'll talk to her. The guitar had some emotional significance Nick here isn't old enough to understand."

The man shook his head again. "I don't think I can do that. You could go there causing trouble and then where would I be?"

Brian wanted to cause trouble. His fists clenched, and he wanted to smash something, throw something, or punch someone. He sucked in a steadying breath.

"Look," the shopkeeper said, opening the box now freed from Brian's hold. "Let me give the boy his money. He earned it after all. That's how things work around here."

Nick's hand went up, but Brian closed his over it. "We don't want the money."

A tired smile pulled at the man's face. "This is a business I run here, and a business has certain rules. I kept the guitar in the back room for a full week before showing it, thinking you'd come and withdraw the commission. When you didn't, what was I supposed to do? I don't run a storage place."

Brian shoved his unruly hair off his face and stared down at tense fingers so he wouldn't glare at the shopkeeper. After all, he couldn't disagree with anything the man said.

A wizened hand stretched along the top of his. "Look, I wish you'd come sooner. It was a beautiful guitar. All I can tell you is it went to someone who will appreciate it. She takes care of what she's gathered here. A right nice young woman."

"You know her then?" *Hope springs eternal*, Brian thought to himself with a wry twist of his lips. "Can you talk to her?"

The old man was about to shake his head when a higher voice added its plea to Brian's. "Please, Mr. Peterson. Can you? I didn't mean for this to happen; I really didn't."

Mr. Peterson put a hand on Nick's head and ruffled his hair. "I'm sorry, son. I wish things had been different."

Nick stared up at him, and the old man coughed once.

"Well, I suppose there's no harm in asking. If you give me your address, I can pass it to her when I see her next. Then she can decide if she wants to find out what's going on."

"Tell her I'll buy her another guitar if she wants, a decent one," Brian threw in.

Mr. Peterson pulled out a pile of bills. "You still have to take this, though. The sale did happen whatever you manage to negotiate with her."

Brian nodded. "Of course. Thanks for your help." He forced down the sarcasm for all he felt it threatening.

The man had tried to help. It wasn't his fault. No, the fault for this mess rested firmly on Brian's shoulders. If he'd talked to Nick about the guitar, the house, about anything real, this would never have happened.

Pulling his lips into a smile, Brian tapped Nick on the shoulder. "How about the pizza?" he asked, determined to keep his promises. Mr. Peterson had been right. Any reasonable parent would have found out about the missing guitar within a week—at least if the guitar was important.

"You two have fun," the shopkeeper called as they headed for the door.

The thought made Brian stumble. He couldn't believe he'd forgotten the most important part.

He glanced down to see Nick's grin. They would have fun. He planned to make sure of it.

Chapter 4

'll never get this," Celia shouted, then glanced around her empty living room, an embarrassed smile tugging at her lips.

"If anyone was listening at the window, I probably scared them off long ago," she said, stroking a hand down the curve of her guitar.

The case held a tuning fork; the book had directions for exactly how to use it. The strings still sounded sour, worse than they'd been when she started. Two days of trying to play, and she had to wreck everything by deciding one string sounded flat. The whole weekend, and she had nothing but a badly tuned guitar to show for it.

Celia strummed once in a feeble hope the tuning had somehow corrected in the moments between when she stopped fiddling with the pegs and now. It hadn't.

"I need a break," she murmured as she carefully lowered the guitar into its case. Then she had to do it all over again because she'd forgotten to put the tuning fork into the little pocket under the neck.

"Who would have thought this was so difficult?"

She rubbed her eyes and grimaced, but she couldn't find any heat to put behind the expression.

Sure, she was frustrated, but she'd never imagined having time to learn something like this before. She wouldn't have dared keep a guitar like this one in her old apartment. Someone would have stolen it in the first week. She still missed the little battery radio she'd kept on her windowsill so she could sing along with the hard rock and rap her charges demanded she know. Someone had stolen it a long time ago.

"Okay, it's not big city entertainment, but I'm going down to the park," she told the empty room. "It'll be light for a while yet."

With a laugh, Celia headed for the door. She'd have to get a cat or something before she gained a reputation even worse than the hermit one she'd been courting.

At the last moment, she grabbed what she'd come to think of as her park pack, a plastic bag filled with chess and checker pieces, and tucked it into the side pocket of her cargo jeans. She just might catch one of the old men who liked to play, though they usually had their own pieces.

The bright sunlight and clean air soon restored Celia's natural optimism, the only reason she'd survived so many years working with homeless and runaway kids. She would figure out the guitar…or maybe she could find someone willing to teach her. It wasn't as if Mr. Peterson found the instrument strange, so there must be some guitar players in Foster's Way. Maybe she could find someone at the bars Melanie kept pushing her to try.

A skip developed in Celia's walk, and she couldn't stop the grin. What she'd been doing was so important, so crucial, she'd never had the chance to consider what it was doing to her. For the first time since running away as a kid, she could relax. She could do things for the fun of it.

When the doctor told Celia how her stressful life had started to damage her heart, aided by a weakness probably inherited from one of her parents, she'd felt betrayed. That had been her life. She had given everything to helping those in circumstances not much different from her own.

Abandoning her purpose had cost Celia on so many levels. She'd defined herself by the counselor role for too many years to let it go easily. But she could see herself adjusting, becoming comfortable here. Content.

Somehow, the picture didn't seem as rosy as she'd hoped.

Celia pushed the thought away, increasing her pace when the old-style horse hitches bordering the park appeared ahead of her. A few bicycles stood against them, and she suspected the structures had never held anything else. Still, they gave the park a quaint feel, as if it had fingers stretching all the way into the past. She liked that about Foster's Way.

Celia stepped onto the asphalt path and headed for the swings. She never saw any other adults on them, but she hadn't outgrown the thrill of flying through the air and hoped she never would. Of course, maybe she hadn't outgrown the thrill because she'd rediscovered it recently.

The bikes she had admired had spilled children onto the small play yard. All the swings were full, and she couldn't just claim a spot. For all she enjoyed the swings, she knew they were meant for a younger crowd.

Celia turned toward the basketball hoops, not really interested in the game, but so she could scan all the children. What had once taken effort—to look beyond herself—had become instinct.

A smile tugged her cheek when she checked out the kids here, though.

If they had ragged clothing, it was from playing hard. Often enough, the tears were patched with bright colors, at least on the younger children. Then there were others clearly in their Sunday best but playing just as hard as anyone else. They weren't afraid of what would happen when they went home. Sure, maybe they would be punished or yelled at, but nothing more terrifying. Nothing to make them run.

She knew the town had a suicide hotline, and a battered women's shelter, but they'd be foolish not to. Here, though, the shelter had no waiting list and the hotline was a phone call to the local clinic. Whatever else might happen behind closed doors, parents didn't chuck their kids out to wander the park, hungry, lonely, and desperate. The kids who ran away, most of them at least, probably changed their minds at the end of the block.

Celia turned toward the chess tables and froze, her stomach curdling. She forced herself to take a deep breath and examine the situation before charging toward the little boy with slumped shoulders. Most likely the other kids had pushed him away and he was sulking. No matter her fears, he probably didn't hunch over the table to hide bruises on his face.

"Hi there." She slipped onto the stone bench opposite him. "Would you like a game?"

He glanced up, and she searched his face for any hint of abuse, unable to stop herself. His rumpled sandy hair made her fingers itch to straighten it, but his serious expression made her revise her age estimate. She'd thought maybe seven, but now she figured he just had a small build.

"I don't have any pieces," the boy said with just a hint of attitude.

Preteen, then, from her experience.

As much as Celia wished she could stop the automatic catalog, she couldn't. She just tried to ignore the commentary as she stuck out her hand.

"I'm Celia."

For a heartbeat, she thought he would pretend not to see her gesture, then the boy shrugged and put his slim hand inside hers.

"Nick."

Pulling out her best grin, Celia said, "Well, Nick, you're in luck today. I came prepared just in case some grand champion happened to be waiting here for a challenge."

He looked up at her, and she could practically hear the "she's weird" running through his mind.

"I'm no grand champion," was all he said.

Celia nodded. "To be honest, I'm not much of a challenge either." She pulled the bag out of her pocket and dropped it onto the table. "So, will you play? Or do you just want to watch me move the pieces around the board so you can laugh."

Again, he gave her that "are you serious?" look, and she returned it with her most innocuous expression.

"Can we play checkers instead?"

His question surprised her because she'd thought he would break away, but Celia covered it up by dumping out the pieces. "Sure. Let's see how many kings you can get."

They played a game, and when she won, both of them started setting up the next without saying anything. Celia tried all the stupid jokes she'd picked up from the shelter kids, and sometimes Nick even laughed, but she noticed how he still seemed glum.

The sun had warmed her back when she sat down, but now shadows stretched from the trees across their table. Celia shivered and looked up, surprised to notice how late it had become.

"Gotcha!"

She glanced at the table more to see what had brought excitement to Nick's tone than because of the game. She looked from one piece to another, and none of her kings or normal pieces could move without Nick swallowing them up. "You won a bit too easily, I think. Here I was reassuring you, when you should have warned me."

He laughed, the sound easy and natural. Whatever sat so heavy on his shoulders didn't seem like abuse, but she couldn't help wondering anyway.

"It's getting dark, and I have to head home now," she said, not wanting him to stay out too late.

"Just one more game. Please?"

Despite the puppy-dog look Nick sent her, she shook her head. "I don't know if I can find my way back in the dark." Celia laughed to show she was joking. "Tell you what. I'll walk you home, and we can talk."

Nick pulled away from the table and his hands froze. She glanced at him. An all too familiar haunted look had taken over his face.

He didn't want her to know where he lived. He might not show the signs of abuse, but at least his residence embarrassed the boy.

She squinted at the sunset as if seeing it for the first time. "Oh, it's later than I thought. Maybe you should go on your own. I wouldn't want to put your father or mother out by having to drive me home."

He stared at her for a few seconds, his eyes squinting as if he tried to read a deeper meaning into her words. Then, he nodded, relief showing in the way his shoulders relaxed and his hands unclenched.

"Yeah, my dad's probably too busy," Nick said, scooping up a handful of pieces. "But maybe I'll see you around the park again sometime?"

The hint of wistful longing underneath his words tugged at her heart in a way so different from the shelter kids she wanted to hug him.

Instead, she shrugged. "I come here a bit, so you might."

"Great." A rare flash of enthusiasm showed in his expression for just a moment, reminding her of the loneliness she'd sensed when she first saw him. "But you'd better get going. Dark falls quickly around here."

Celia nodded and tucked the now full bag away. "See you around sometime."

She wanted to find a place and watch him leave just to make sure. Night fell very late in the summer months, and he'd probably missed curfew…if he had parents who cared about that sort of thing. But she had few friends and didn't want to betray his trust. She'd keep an eye out for him when she came down to the park, but she couldn't spy on Nick. That would be too close to stalking for comfort, especially considering they were chance-met strangers.

Sharing a game of checkers was one thing. Trailing him was another, whatever her worries.

Brian swung the sledgehammer at the last piece of the room divider, and it collapsed in a cloud of plaster. He pulled the dust mask from his face and laughed.

"Nick, come see. The wall's down."

Though his son had shown no interest in the process, he had to want to see the destruction's aftermath. Brian didn't care how upset the boy might be. This was wonderful.

Nick didn't appear.

Brian tried brushing the plaster dust from his shirt and pants, but gave it up as futile. He'd require a shower and his clothes a beating outside before they'd be safe in the laundry.

"Nick? Where are you?"

Again, silence greeted him. He'd thought they'd moved forward, even laughing together over pizza the other night and exploring parts of the town yesterday. Nick had looked a little glum this morning, but Brian expected that. After all, his son had lost his mother only two months ago. Brian just hadn't expected to be the target of the glumness any more.

He sighed and ran a hand through his hair, the long strands tangling in his fingers. He worked them free, only then realizing how the plaster dust had clung to his hands, too. His mouth twisted into a grimace, white-coated hair falling into his face. What was the character in Peanuts called? Pigpen?

He knew which one he resembled in that moment, and it certainly wasn't the disembodied voice of a parent.

Brian glanced at the wall again, or rather the absence of wall, and his grimace changed into a grin. The wallpaper had been grueling, but this was pure fun. Did boys ever really grow out of the destructive phase?

The thought brought him back to his missing son.

Brian stamped his feet hard, trying one last time to dislodge the plaster before he left a trail through the house. Brilliant colors caught his attention. He looked out the window, surprised to see the beginning of a summer sunset.

"We should have eaten hours ago," he muttered, wondering if that was why Nick gave him the cold shoulder. He'd wanted to finish this step in one day, but dismantling the wall someone had added to split the large parlor into two rooms had taken longer than he'd expected.

As if anything in this process had gone as planned.

"Nick. Where are you hiding? Are you as hungry as I am?"

Brian reached Nick's room even as he called. He pushed the door open, but the room stood empty. He found the same in the kitchen, the basement, his room, and the attic. As much as he tried, Brian couldn't keep the frustrated anger from his tone. Not that it mattered. He searched every room, the backyard, and finally the front.

Nick was nowhere.

Brian sat on the front steps, thinking hard and trying not to panic. He'd moved them to Foster's Way in part because the low crime rate meant Nick could be a kid. He could go out on his own without an escort and have the freedom to come to terms with the changes in his life.

But knowing this didn't ease the worry churning in Brian's gut. Foster's Way was safer, but not safe. Nick needed to show some street smarts. He needed to be home by nightfall at least, earlier in these bright summer evenings.

A smile tugged at his cheek, and Brian shook his head.

Nick wouldn't really be in trouble. He probably just missed how late it had become. Brian hadn't noticed either, and he was supposed to be the responsible adult.

Still, when darkness did fall, it came quickly. Brian knew he wouldn't be able to settle down with Nick missing no matter how innocent the cause. He'd go down to the park five blocks from their house. Nick had mentioned the checkers tables there. Maybe he found someone to play with.

Brian stared out across the street for another minute as he reviewed his son's comment and sighed. He'd been so caught up in getting the house ready he'd missed his cue. When Nick brought up the checkers, he should have offered to go with his son.

This parenting gig was harder than any stage he'd ever played.

He turned back into the house and grabbed a jacket to cover the state of his clothes. It was an army discard he'd worn since before graduating high school. Nick would be in the park for sure, and all Brian had to do was play one game. Parenting wasn't so hard. He just had to remember to listen.

Falling into a comfortable stride, Brian let a smile creep over his features. It seemed like a stupid thing to make him happy—Nick being lost—but the worry he'd felt meant he'd recovered something Kaitlin had stolen all those years before.

When she first denied him access, he'd done everything to fight it until his mother had pulled him aside and pointed out the fighting only hurt Nick. Mom believed Kaitlin would come around, but she never did. Self-preservation made Brian push all thoughts of Nick, including worry, away. He'd lost himself in the music world.

He stamped both feet harder than before, annoyed at the intrusion from the ghost of his ex-wife. Some might consider her will a sign she regretted what she'd done, but he didn't. He would have been there in a heartbeat if she'd ever offered him time with Nick. The will felt more like casting their son away, no matter how grateful Brian had been to make the catch.

A cloud of dust rose to cover even his jacket as anger sent his feet pounding against the concrete sidewalk. His throat tickled until he coughed to clear it. He'd accepted this responsibility without hesitation, but his son had been less willing.

Running off like this without saying anything mocked all Brian had done since the funeral. Nick would have some explaining to do, and this better not happen again. Brian should have been cleaning up the mess in the parlor...and on him...not tracking Nick down.

His stomach grumbled its own annoyance, no longer distracted by the heavy swing of the hammer. He should have had supper coming, too, instead of searching the streets.

The toe of his sneakers caught on a crack in the pavement, and he stumbled, a curse ripping from his mouth loud enough to bring the neighbors down on him.

Brian let the anger sweep over him until both fists clenched with the force of it. He clung to his anger in an almost desperate attempt to hide from the fear that Nick wouldn't be in the park. If he wasn't, where would Brian look next?

As far as he knew, his son had no friends, and though Foster's Way seemed a nice town, all places had their own dangerous elements. Nick was only twelve.

Chapter 5

Celia glanced toward the tables when she reached the park entrance and sighed. The boy hadn't listened. He'd sat there again, staring at the distance with his shoulders slumped. She wanted to go over, to force him to go home no matter how little the place appealed to him, but she wasn't his parent. She was no more than a stranger.

She shrugged.

This wasn't the city. The kids on the block where she lived stayed out late playing in the street, their only light whatever spilled from front windows with curtains pulled back.

Life was different here. She just had to adapt.

The stern lecture didn't have any effect on the tension in her chest, but she had no choice. Another sigh whispered out, and head bent, she turned onto her path home.

A large foot broke her view of the pavement, and Celia stumbled, her leg knocking painfully into one of the horse hitches. She followed the long leg up to find a lanky man in front of her. Dust clouds rose from his baggy, military-cut jacket, and his dark hair hung long and loose around his shoulders.

Celia shuddered, her city training screaming danger.

She drew in a breath to call for help, then paused.

Despite his neglected appearance, no stench rose from the man, not of alcohol or even just the smell of old sweat. Celia coughed as his dust reached the back of her throat. It jolted her into awareness.

This wasn't the city, and whatever he looked like, he wasn't some derelict, a potentially unbalanced man. She'd been staring like a victim waiting for the gun to go off.

Celia shook her head and muttered, "Sorry," before she realized he'd been staring just as much as she had.

He could have left, could have ducked around her, could have said something to break her concentration or calm her fears.

She couldn't stop herself from taking another look now that her preconceptions had given way. He had a strong face with laugh lines beside both eyes, but something told her he hadn't used them much in recent times. His broad shoulders matched a tall, lanky frame. Most men stood taller than Celia, but he would have risen above many of them.

She wondered what it would feel like to have his arms around her.

A blush heated her neck and cheeks, and she ducked her head, doubly embarrassed now with this new behavior and her runaway thoughts. She stepped around him and forced her feet one in front of the other as they took her away from this situation.

Surely she wasn't so desperate for company. First she befriended a lonely boy, and now she'd caught herself eyeing complete strangers.

Maybe she should take Melanie up on her offer. Picking up a guy in a bar didn't sound any more appealing, but at least they'd have small talk to fill the awkward silences.

BRIAN STARED AFTER THE YOUNG woman, something about her walk familiar. He smiled, remembering first her shock then the spark of interest. He hadn't meant to startle her, but she'd turned too quickly for him to move out of the way. Still, he couldn't find it in himself to regret the encounter, as brief as it had been. If nothing else, it pushed away his lingering anger...and the fear it hid. He still had to get Nick, though.

He turned back to the park and scanned the play structure, the swing, the basketball hoops, and finally found the tables

Nick had mentioned. No other kids remained in the park, and he recognized Nick's small frame the moment he found the boy, sitting at the farthest table.

A coil of tension in his chest he'd tried to ignore unwound at the sight of his son. Relief mixed with frustration and anger until he found both fists clenched at his side.

"Nick."

Whether from surprise or the anger in Brian's voice, Nick jerked around so quickly he almost fell off the stone bench. The growing shadows hid the boy's face, but Brian couldn't mistake his words.

"You came. I thought you weren't going to."

Something softened in Brian's heart, and his anger drained away as he loped across the remaining space between them. He ruffled the untidy mop of hair on Nick's head and almost growled, "I didn't know I was invited."

Brian drew in a deep breath and sank onto the bench opposite Nick. "You scared me. I was working on the wall and lost track of time. Then I went to look for you, and you were gone."

Nick stared down at his hands. "I *told* you I was going to the park," he mumbled.

Brian dragged a hand through his hair. "That was hours ago."

"Am I in trouble?"

The contrast between the quiet voice and the excitement of moments before burned Brian. He reached across and put a hand on Nick's shoulder. "No, not this time. But I need you to tell me...and make sure I know. And I don't want you out alone this late, alright?"

He almost laughed at the words he'd never intended to say. Brian could remember yelling at his dad that his kids would never have a curfew or anything to keep them from the fun.

Nick looked up at him from beneath heavy bangs. "Does this mean you're not angry?"

"Not anymore. But I was very worried."

His son nodded, then tilted his head to one side as if considering what Brian had said. "So will you play checkers with me?"

Brian looked at the empty board. The table was stone without any sign of a drawer for pieces.

"Oh," Nick said. "The lady had them."

Brian didn't have to ask to know which woman his son had met. He wanted to give Nick the whole stranger warning, but instead, the hint of vanilla that had risen from her skin came back to him. He traced her features with his mind's eye, compelled to savor. No, it didn't surprise him at all to learn she'd captured his son as well.

He laughed.

Like father like son. The first woman to tweak his curiosity since his marriage with Kaitlin had failed, and it was a chance meeting outside a park without even the exchange of names. He hadn't been celibate. Women on the road were happy to spend a little time in his bed without expectations. He hadn't relaxed around them enough to want more than just the comfort of a warm body.

Nick was looking at him a little strangely when he glanced at his son, but Brian just shook his head. "She didn't say her name, did she?"

The boy nodded. "Celia."

"Celia what?" Brian asked even as he thought the short, elegant name suited her well.

"Just Celia. She played checkers with me when no one else would, but she had to go home cause it was getting dark."

Brian laughed again, this time at Nick's innocence. He'd bet the woman had been trying to send Nick home without being obvious.

Then he remembered what she'd been doing when he almost bumped into her. She'd been staring at these tables.

"She didn't ask you to go with her, did she?" His heart accelerated at the thought. Why else would a grown woman be hanging out in a park? There'd been no kids with her after all.

Nick shook his head. "Oh no. She didn't. She offered to walk me home, but... I didn't want to go yet."

Relief swept Brian only to be followed with a wave of disappointment. If she had walked Nick home, he wouldn't have been there anyway. He'd have been out looking for his son.

At least it seemed she wasn't a predator or something like one. He'd never had to worry about that sort of thing before, and it felt odd to think of people in this way.

"She probably thought I was the danger," he muttered, remembering the plaster and his uncut hair. No wonder her first reaction had more to do with fear than interest.

"What?" Nick asked, but the boy's attention was back on the board.

Not wanting to disappoint his son, Brian said, "Hey, why don't you get enough stones and we can still play."

Nick shrugged. "You wouldn't be able to tell which colors they were."

Brian reached for a solution, staring at the board as if it would grow pieces if he looked hard enough. It didn't, but the white powder cascading from his clothes to mark the board did give him an idea.

"You get the stones. I'll make the colors," he said with a laugh. All this plaster dust had to be worth something.

They played two more games, the board getting a coating of what looked like snow by the time they were halfway through the second.

"Hey, that's my piece," Brian said, when Nick pushed a stone onto Brian's back row.

"It had white on it. That means it's mine."

Brian couldn't help smiling when he saw Nick's grin. His son made short work of the few pieces still clear of the powder he had shaken from his clothes. "Next time we play with real pieces."

"Deal." Nick gave another of his grins and added, "I won."

Stretching both hands above his head, Brian squinted toward their street. Few streetlamps marked the roads, unnecessary where cars were rare and most people didn't go out at night. Down at the other side of town where there were bars and late night coffee houses. He could see the splash of light blocking the stars.

Brian stood up and turned his back on those lights. He'd given up that life.

"Come on, Nick. We need to head home and find something to eat. I'm starving."

As if on cue, Nick's stomach let out a loud rumble.

They both laughed as they left the park, his son scrambling to keep up with Brian's stride.

When they crossed the line of hitching posts where he'd last seen her, Celia drifted into Brian's mind.

It had been so long since a woman hovered in his thoughts he didn't know what to do with the feeling. He wanted to know more about her, to see her smile. The last woman he allowed himself to care about had handed him his walking papers some ten years ago.

Brian shrugged and slowed down so Nick wouldn't have to work so hard. He'd probably never see her again, so he should just put her out of his mind.

Chapter 6

Celia stretched her back as she walked home. They'd had a slow day up front, not uncommon for a Monday, and so had worked on unloading a new shipment. Her fingers still felt gritty from the cardboard dust and paper powder clinging to the new books, but she'd enjoyed the work.

Melanie had been in full swing about a musician she'd heard with some friends over the weekend. Celia laughed aloud as she remembered the young woman's enthusiasm. Had she ever been enthralled with a touch of fame like that?

Celia knew she'd never had the chance. She envied her friend for only a moment before realizing she had all the opportunities in the world now. She only needed to take advantage of them.

"You sure are looking happy today, Miss Baker."

Celia turned her smile on Mr. Peterson and waved a hello. "How could I not be with all this sunshine?" she asked, pointing toward the blue sky.

"Some folks would say it's hot and sticky."

"Some folks don't know how to enjoy a good thing," she answered in a mimicry of his wording.

Mr. Peterson shook his head. "Ain't that the truth."

Instead of the returning smile she'd expected, he frowned. "You have a moment? I need to talk to you about something."

If he'd shown even a hint of a smile, Celia would have rushed into the store, sure he'd found her a treasure. Her chest tightened, though she couldn't imagine what would have put such a serious expression on the man's face.

"Of course," she said, keeping her tone steady with effort as she followed him in.

He crossed behind the counter, straightened the boxes there, used his apron to dust the clean surface, and did anything he could to avoid her gaze.

Finally, her chest aching even more, she dropped a hand on top of his to still his movement. "What is it, Mr. Peterson? Just tell me. It can't be that awful."

Even as the words slipped from her mouth, a heavy weight settled on her. If it wasn't, why would Mr. Peterson behave this way?

The old man coughed twice, then brushed a hand over his face and sank onto the stool behind the counter. "No good in keeping it from you. I'm a bit embarrassed how this all came about. I shouldn't even be bothering you with this, but I promised and he was just a boy. A sad, little boy."

Celia shook her head, unable to understand but worried somehow Mr. Peterson had found an abused kid for her to help even here.

He raised his head to stare at her. "You remember the guitar I sold you?"

She fought to draw in a breath, her chest so tight she could hardly gasp out, "It was stolen?"

All her years in the depths of the city and now she trafficked in stolen goods? Here, in the place she wanted to make her haven away from that world?

Mr. Peterson grabbed her hand, pulling her against the glass shelving beneath the counter in his effort to comfort. "Now, Miss Baker. Don't you go panicking or anything. Take a deep breath. There, there. See, it's not as bad as all that."

The darkness at the edges of her vision slowly brightened, but her heart still stumbled. She clung to Mr. Peterson's voice and the touch of his dry, callused fingers on hers. A trembling smile tugged at her lips as she struggled to pull herself together.

"Of course not. Of course," she managed, her tone faint and whispery.

"Do you need to sit down?"

She looked up into his concerned expression and forced her heart to slow, her chest to release. She forced calm to settle over her.

"No," Celia said in a more normal tone. "No, I'm fine. Just a little surprised, that's all."

He shook his head. "I shouldn't have told you that way. I just didn't know how to say it and so made it seem worse than it is."

Celia turned her hand so she could squeeze Mr. Peterson's, trying not to wonder what he was telling her. "It's alright. I get this way every once in a while. It's why I left the city. I'll be fine in a minute."

He pulled his hand away, the concern on his face not eased. "At least let me get you a glass of water. Shouldn't have given you a scare."

She shook her head. "No, just tell me." Her lips quirked up into a smile. "The curiosity is killing me."

She didn't add "literally," though she thought it when her heart stumbled over another beat. "What's wrong with the guitar?"

"Nothing's wrong with it, exactly. Only the boy who owned it didn't get permission from his dad to sell, and his dad isn't happy. They both agree the guitar was the boy's to do with as he wished. That's not the problem. It's just it had some meaning to the dad."

Celia frowned. Not exactly stolen, but not exactly available either.

Only last night, after returning from the park filled with an antsy energy, she'd worked out the tuning fork and managed her first chord. It hadn't sounded beautiful or anything, but the guitar held its tune as best as she could tell and the strings didn't buzz too much. The sense of victory washed over her again now just thinking about it.

"He wants it back, doesn't he?" Her voice came out flat, dull. She'd grown attached to the instrument in the short time it had shared her cottage. The guitar had become a challenge she was determined to conquer, and she didn't want to give up the feeling.

"Well, Miss Baker, he does; yes, he does. But you bought it fair and square. I almost didn't even tell you about it. The sparkle in your eyes when you picked it out of my window, well, it makes the whole collection of objects worth it, if you understand me. Just forget I said anything. The guitar is yours and there's nothing anyone can do about it."

She stared into Mr. Peterson's earnest face. In the short time she'd been browsing his shop, she knew he'd come to think of her as a niece, someone he felt responsible for, someone he saved treasures for. Of course he'd take her side.

She closed her eyes for a moment and remembered the feel of the guitar's neck sinking against her palm. It felt well-loved, cared for. That feeling made up half the attraction it held. And the feeling had been worn into the wood by the man who owned the guitar before her.

A sigh came from her lips as Celia fought the realization she should give it back. She wanted to be selfish; she wanted to keep it. She wanted to treasure the instrument the way it had been treasured in its first home.

"You don't have to," Mr. Peterson repeated, "But they'll repay you what you gave me."

Celia laughed, the sharp sound making the hanging pots ring for a moment. "If only it was just about the money."

Mr. Peterson came round the counter and gave her an awkward pat on the shoulder. "You don't have to make up your mind now. I know you really looked forward to having a guitar. If I had another, I'd offer you a different one, but somehow I don't think it would be the same. Which reminds me. The man offered a replacement though I doubt that changes things."

She smiled at the old man, unsurprised by his understanding. He dealt in treasures, not cast-asides. He understood things weren't interchangeable.

"You think on it a bit," he continued. "If you do decide to give the guitar back, I have his address around here somewhere."

"You have his address?" Somehow the existence of an address, even scratched out on a scrap of paper, made the situation just a little more real. "Can I see it?"

Even she didn't quite understand her request.

Mr. Peterson looked at her for a quiet moment before he went behind the counter. He dug around a bit then pulled out just what she'd expected, a scrap of white, ruled paper, like from a school binder.

Celia brushed the address with one finger, reading the tense handwriting. The anger—upset—revealed by those tight, stiff letters only made her desire to keep the guitar harder to support.

"I'll take this with me, if you don't mind. I still haven't decided, but if I do, there'd be no reason to delay."

Mr. Peterson waved his agreement, but a frown pulled on his wrinkled face until jowls gathered on either side of his chin. "I really am sorry about this. I can just throw it away, you know. You have no obligation at all."

Her mind slipped to the lonely boy she'd met in the park. Somewhere, there was another boy whose father had to be angry with him. What would his dad do? How would he treat the boy who'd given up his precious guitar?

"I know, Mr. Peterson. But it's only fair to think about it, at least." She turned to the door with none of the energy she'd felt when she left the bookstore. Did her selfish desire to keep the guitar weigh against an unhappy kid? Or was she just projecting, and the kid and father had already made up and moved on.

Celia shook her head, knowing she had no objectivity. She'd seen too many abused, neglected boys in her tenure with the runaways even without her own time on the street. The bigger world didn't work that way, did it?

"You have a good day now," Mr. Peterson called from behind her, his tone lacking its normal energy as well.

Celia forced a smile when she glanced back. No reason to burden the old man with her tangles.

"You have a good day too, Mr. Peterson. And don't worry. This will all work out." She added "somehow" under her breath, wondering if she could uncover the true situation.

What if the father had just been upset at not being asked? The guitar hadn't been in perfect tune or she'd never have tried the tuning fork. Didn't that mean it hadn't been played for months at least? Maybe Mr. Peterson had misunderstood, and it was lack of control upsetting the father, not the guitar's loss, though why would they have left an address in that case.

Her thoughts went round in circles, plaguing her all the rest of the way home and preventing her from enjoying the sunshine. She rushed her steps, wanting to see the guitar again as if it would have all the answers, even as she knew if it held secrets, it wouldn't reveal them to her.

Chapter 7

B rian took a deep swig of his root beer and grinned, using a hand to wipe some of the brown liquid from the corner of his mouth. It had taken half the day, but they'd cleaned up the parlor. They now had one big room to play with.

He did a quick air guitar riff to celebrate then glanced around to share the victory, but Nick had left hours before, right after they'd succeeded in prying the last of the partition free of the wall. Brian guessed his son got enough satisfaction from that.

"Hey, Nick. Come look at this."

He waited a few minutes then took another drink without the same enthusiasm. For all that they'd connected a time or two, Nick still didn't seek out his company. And Brian had caught a glum expression on his son's face many times. Like after he suggested they tackle the next step of the cleaning.

Brian sighed, placing his soda down against the now clean wall before turning to the stairs. He'd tried to give his son time to come to terms with what happened, but just how much time would Nick need? Brian didn't expect Nick to forget his mother and let it all go this quickly, but he'd hoped they'd be friends at least by now.

Friends who talked.

Part of him wondered if he should have accepted custody. Maybe Nick would have been happier with his grandparents or aunt, but he'd had his son taken away from him once, and he wouldn't let it happen again, not even to make his mother happy.

His feet pounded on the uncarpeted, wood stairs, loud enough to warn the neighbors he was coming much less Nick. He didn't want to give his son any chance to claim Brian had surprised him or intruded, but at the same time he didn't want Nick moping all day.

Maybe he'd needed to take a more direct approach from the start.

The sound of his knock against the doorframe seemed loud in the small hallway, but Nick didn't even look up from the electronic game he was playing while stretched out on his bed.

"Nick?" Brian kept the frustration from his voice with effort. "Why don't you put the game away and come see what I've done?"

His son grunted, just enough sign to prove he'd heard, but nothing useful.

Brian forced clenched fingers to relax and decided the grunt served as an invitation. He crossed the room and sank onto the bed, eliciting another grunt when his weight shifted Nick.

The room seemed unnaturally clean. Everything lay carefully placed on shelves as it had been when Nick first moved in. Brian wondered if Nick was just the neatest young boy in the country, or whether his son never read or played with anything except the handheld.

A frown pinched Brian's forehead as his frustrated anger at Kaitlin returned.

This was his son. He should know these things; he should know all about Nick. But he didn't.

"Hey," he tried again. "I finished cleaning up the plaster. The room is huge. Can you help me figure out how we'll use it? It's just the two of us after all. You should have some say."

Nick grunted again without looking up.

Brian forced back the need to shake his son and pulled his lips into a smile. "We could put in a bowling alley. Or make it over with a huge train set." He pulled the most outrageous ideas out, hoping to get some reaction. "Why don't we put in an Olympic-sized swimming pool?"

Nick didn't even glance his way.

Through Nick's earbuds, Brian could hear the tinny echo of game music.

"I got him!" Nick yelled, startling Brian almost off the bed.

"Were you even listening?" Brian demanded.

Before he could think it through, he wrapped his fingers around the headphone cords and tugged.

The earbuds came free with a popping sound, and music poured out clearly, the setting way too high.

"You'll go deaf like that," he said, not missing the irony when his father had told him the same thing after he got his first amplified guitar with money saved up from summer jobs.

Nick stared down at the machine still, but sharp lines appeared on his forehead.

Brian didn't care anymore. He'd worked hard all day, and now Nick had tarnished every bit of satisfaction.

He would have his son's respect if nothing else. Brian snatched the game, jerking it out of Nick's hands.

"Hey! You'll make me lose. Give it back."

Nick grabbed for the box, but Brian held it easily out of reach. A flash of guilt rushed through him at using a bully's tactics, but how else was he to get Nick to pay attention?

"It's just a game. You can play it whenever. I want us to talk now."

Nick sat up and folded his arms across his chest. "Fine then. Talk."

Brian ignored Nick's glower as best he could. This had gone too far for him to back down. He couldn't let Nick get away with this behavior, but at the same time, he wished they could return to those moments when they'd actually connected with none of the bitterness that seemed to radiate from Nick now.

"Look, I just want you to have some input in the house. It's your home, too, you know. We could do some fun things here."

Nick scowled. "It's not my home. I didn't want to live here. You do whatever you want."

Brian clenched his fist and drew in a slow breath. "It is your home. This house won't ever replace what you had before, but we both need to get used to it. This is going to be our life now. Doesn't it make sense to make it yours?"

Nick shook his head, and Brian held back a sigh. Maybe he was going about this all wrong. After all, he'd swept into Nick's life out of nowhere. If he didn't know what Nick wanted or liked, Nick had no way of knowing who he was either.

Brian shifted so they were sitting side by side and tried to take Nick's hand in his.

His son jerked free, clenching both hands together in his lap.

"I know this is a big change for you. It's a big one for me, too," Brian said. "After the divorce, I never really expected to try again. To settle down, I mean." He stopped, stunned.

Brian hadn't realized the truth until that moment. All his restlessness made sense in this context. The only other time he'd tried to make a home, Kaitlin had torn it from his grasp, so he never took the chance again until now.

He drew in a steadying breath and let his mouth twist up into a half-grin. "I thought I'd just stay on the music circuit until my voice got too scratchy and no one bought my albums anymore. Then I'd buy a spot in an island paradise somewhere my joints wouldn't ache and beautiful women would bring me colorful drinks. Pretty silly, huh?"

Nick met his sideways glance with an expression devoid of humor.

Brian shrugged. "I guess you're not old enough yet for that pipedream. For me, it was all about the music."

Nick shoved off the bed, startling Brian into a quick, "What?" before he turned on his father.

"You could have left me with my aunt. You gave me the guitar so you would enjoy spending time with me doing what you like. You're just trying to make me feel guilty. You think I don't know how you pretend to play the guitar just to poke at me. You gave it to me fair and square. I didn't ask you to, I didn't want it, and so I got rid of it. Just like you're going to get rid of me. Mom always said you didn't have a settling bone in your body. You couldn't settle for a house, a wife, and certainly not a kid. Well, I don't want to be here, either!"

Brian stepped back, stunned, his mind snapping to the moment Nick's attitude had changed this very morning. It hadn't been about not wanting to work. Where another would shout hurrah, he'd played the air guitar. He'd always done the gesture since before he was old enough to play a real one. He hadn't meant anything by it.

Nick didn't give him time to wrap his mind around this new understanding. His son grabbed a jacket from the hook behind the door and took off.

Brian's fingers curled, and he stared down at them.

He hadn't been trying to make Nick guilty. And he certainly didn't intend to run off. He hadn't run off in the first place.

"Thanks a lot, Kaitlin. Even now you're still ruining my relationship with Nick."

The words hung before him, and he flushed a little, an awkward feeling coming over him as it had every time he talked to her ghost. They'd talked more in the months since her death than in the same number of years before it. But he only got echoes from the past. No answers, no explanations, and certainly no help.

He pushed off the bed then paused. The game lay toward the edge of the bed where he'd dropped it, headphone cords tangled already. Brian untangled the cords, lowered the volume, and put the game onto Nick's pillow, hoping his son would accept the unspoken apology.

How could the two of them form a lasting relationship with so much poison just waiting to boil up between them? How many years had Kaitlin spent filling Nick's mind with lies? He wanted to confront her with the truth. Her unfounded jealousy drove them apart, not any action on his part.

But he couldn't, and he certainly wouldn't win any points with Nick by slandering the boy's mother now. No, he had to figure out a way to prove she'd been wrong with his actions. That would be the only way to bring Nick around. He had to stop hiding in the house and become part of this life.

Brian headed down the stairs, thoughtful. He needed to make the effort, to find some kids for Nick to play with, meet some people, and make connections here. Maybe then Nick would be able to believe he didn't plan to disappear from Nick's life like Kaitlin had.

A smile grew as a wisp of memory teased Brian.

He could think of one person he'd like to meet. The woman at the park: Celia.

She could turn out to be a prissy, bound up lady with no thoughts of her own, but somehow he doubted it. She'd gone down to the park by herself. That showed a youthful spirit, while playing checkers with Nick showed kindness.

If she had been alone.

He pushed the thought of her having a husband and kids away, enjoying his fantasy even as he went back to work on the house. He'd wait Nick out and then they'd talk about how to make this house, and this town, a home both of them wanted to live in.

Chapter 8

Celia strummed the strings one more time, her grin broadening. "Three chords. Enough to play a song," she told the guitar. Then she laughed. "Well, a simple song."

She'd been practicing ever since she got home, trying not to think.

Her hands stroked the length of the neck. "I wonder what you sang before."

Celia shook her head and lifted the guitar off her lap. Now she'd started talking to the instrument. It was quickly becoming more than just an object to her.

A twinge of guilt made her wince as memory of her conversation with Mr. Peterson that afternoon rose despite her best efforts. The more the instrument became like a person, the more its past haunted her.

She tucked the guitar into its case, smoothing the shoulder strap around the body so the lid would close without jamming.

Could she keep it? Could she deny the history burned into every smooth spot on the wood, history created by a man who hadn't been ready to let go?

Celia wanted to deny the guilt; she wanted to keep this treasure, to keep the feeling of exhilaration each success brought her.

"It's only a guitar," she muttered. "You can always buy another."

The words came out as flat as the feelings behind them. Any other guitar wouldn't be this one. Its sense of history was half the reason she kept pushing. She longed to play the guitar as it deserved, as its past owner had. What kind of history would an assembly-line one hold?

She wanted to laugh at her own contradictions. She wanted to pretend the past didn't matter, but it did.

Running from her ghosts had become a pattern for her, and this time proved no different.

She found herself grabbing the bag of pieces again, carefully avoiding the scrap of paper she'd dropped on the table when she got home.

Maybe Nick would be at the park. Or if not, maybe some other kid or even a grown up. She hoped time spent with a real person would stop this silliness about the guitar. If it didn't mean the sum total of her life outside work, surely it wouldn't have as much impact.

The sunshine worked its magic as it usually did, and before she even reached the hitching posts, the bounce had returned to Celia's step. She could swing if she couldn't find someone to play chess or checkers. She could even challenge herself.

Celia laughed aloud at the thought. It wouldn't be much of an effort. She was a mediocre player in the first place. The game could go on forever in a dance of back and forth that never ended in a checkmate.

She glanced toward the tables, and her pace accelerated at the sight of Nick. She'd recognize his sandy hair and slim arms anywhere.

"Come to recoup your losses?" Celia dropped the bag onto the table in front of him.

Instead of questioning her memory when he'd been the winner of their games, Nick just shrugged.

She stepped around him to settle on the opposite bench, bringing his face into view. If anything, he seemed even glummer than the last time. Then, she'd sensed loneliness. Now, there seemed like something more.

Celia pulled out the pieces and separated chess from checkers to give herself time to think.

Nick turned to sit fully on the bench and snagged the black checkers one after another, setting up his side of the board.

"You want to go first?" she asked, sweeping the chess pieces into the bag.

"You go," he said, his voice gruff.

Celia glanced up and stared at him for a moment, but he didn't say anything. She sighed inwardly. A tough little guy. She'd seen more than her share of those.

The pieces shuffled across the board, slowly changing color balance until almost all her red pieces were off to the side. Celia managed to get a king, but after the third jump, he sideswiped it, and not even with a king of his own.

She laughed. "I should have seen that coming."

He gave her a serious nod rather than the grin she'd expected and turned his focus onto the game. Four more moves, and he'd won soundly. "Again?"

She set out her pieces as an answer and waited for him to make the first move before she asked, "So what's keeping you down?"

He jerked his gaze to hers, and his eyes narrowed. She thought for a moment he wouldn't answer, then he said only, "My dad's angry with me," before looking down again.

Celia put her hand on his arm and gave it a squeeze, before leaning back to her side of the table. "That's rough. It's not because I kept you out late last night, is it?"

He shook his head and curled his shoulders as though he wanted to shrink inside himself.

She grew still, all her senses on alert.

She'd seen the move too many times before, a defensive posture. "How angry is he?"

Celia knew the right questions, but what had been a straight-forward interview at the shelter seemed wrong here.

"Pretty pissed," Nick muttered without looking up. "I did something…"

Celia shook her head. "It's not your fault," she burst out. "Grownups should control their tempers whatever you do."

He looked at her then, and she met his gaze steadily.

"Does he hurt you, Nick? Is that why you're hiding out here? Is that why you didn't want me to bring you home?"

A flush tinged his skin, and Nick slashed an arm across the forgotten board, sending the pieces scattering across the grass.

"My father would never do anything like that!" he shouted. "How could you say so? You don't know him. You don't know what he's done for me. You just leave him alone. Leave me alone."

Celia jerked away, stunned.

She watched Nick scramble off the bench and stomp away, unable to come up with words of apology to make it up to him. She hadn't meant to slander his dad. She'd just been trying to help.

He kicked one of the hitching posts as he passed, and Nick's angry stride developed an awkward hop, but he didn't slow down. Celia's gaze stayed with him until he turned off the tree-lined street.

Celia chastised herself the whole time.

She'd moved here to get away from the city and all it meant. So why did she go looking for aspects of her old life in her new one? She had to insult the only friend she'd made outside of work besides Mr. Peterson. Why assume Nick had been abused? Could she never let go of the life she'd led? Why couldn't she accept the people around her now didn't have poison welling up inside?

While she searched out the pieces in the grass, then remade the board to make sure she'd found every one, the questions kept pushing at her. Could she put the past behind her and start a new life? Or would she lock herself up in the cottage so she didn't have to interact with anyone but herself and a guitar? A guitar that held more guilt than pleasure ever since she'd learned about another sad little boy.

She'd been so confident in her ability to start again. Had her confidence been misplaced?

Celia laughed, the bitter sound a further sign Nick had passed his bad mood to her. Was she willing to give up so easily?

She just needed to try harder, that's all. And she needed to apologize to Nick the very next time she saw him. What did she know about his father or his life? Nothing.

WHEN CELIA GOT HOME FROM the park, the space seemed empty. Yells and shouts from the neighborhood children reached through the window, but instead of filling the room, they only emphasized how no one shared her cottage—or her life. How could she have messed up so thoroughly? Her coworkers at the shelter often praised her perception. Where had her skills gone?

Celia sighed as she crossed to the kitchen and filled the kettle.

She didn't know how to interact with real people. It had been so long. Maybe that's why she preferred going through the boxes and sorting the new books. Maybe it wasn't the discovery but rather the break from people whose motives she couldn't tell at a glance.

She slumped into one of the kitchen chairs, metal and plastic constructs from an earlier decade. The polka-dotted cushion creaked with the pressure.

If she hid from the customers, from Melanie, how could she go out and make real contact with her town and her world?

Her gaze fell on the guitar, its case just visible through the open kitchen door.

She laughed as an absurd thought crossed her mind. "I don't think pinning my hopes on a music career is any way to meet people," she told the instrument even as she rose and walked toward it. "No one will be clamoring to hear me play any time soon."

The kettle's whistle drew her back from her objective, and she occupied her hands with the process of making tea. The simple steps did not distract her thoughts, though, and the out-landish idea of music opening doors just wouldn't leave.

Celia sank down into the chair again, both hands wrapped around the mug, its warmth comforting despite the heat out-side.

"You know," she told the hint of guitar case teasing her. "I could do the open mic night. All I'd need is not to be awful."

She chuckled at the thought of punishing her new neigh-bors, but when she closed her eyes to breathe in the mixed scent of hibiscus and lemon, she saw herself perched on a stool in front of a crowd.

"Did your former owner ever take you out on the town?" She'd meant the question as a joke, but the minute the words left her mouth, Celia's hands clenched around the mug and she stared into the colored liquid rather than at the peeping case.

What if the former owner had? What if this guitar bore the weight of risks taken, chances made? Would a boy have under-stood all that? Would he have understood the baggage shared along with a simple object?

Celia's chest tightened until she struggled to draw a breath. What if the boy she played checkers with in the park had done something like the kid with the guitar? Would he even see the weight of his father's anger? Or would it seem arbitrary and confusing. Nick had certainly been quick to defend his father despite the anger.

She dragged in a steadying breath, but couldn't banish the image of Nick as the boy who'd sold the guitar from her mind.

How could she consider the fragile relationship she might have built up with this construct of wood and strings more im-portant than a boy's relationship with his father? If she felt the guitar's life, how it drew a person, how could she deny the feel-ing to someone who had experienced it so much longer, who had imbued the object with its very life? It seemed selfish.

Her neglected tea sat abandoned on the table as Celia crossed to the guitar. She pulled it from the case and nestled the curved body under her right breast. The open strings hummed with resonance when she stroked them, but she could hear a discordant note beneath.

One string had gone out of tune again.

Even as she identified a physical reason for the sound, Celia sensed the guitar wasn't happy here. It accused her with its only voice. No matter how tenderly she cared for it, she wasn't the one to give it spirit, to give it a soul.

With one last stroke, Celia said goodbye. She had no real choice.

"I'll bring you home tomorrow," she promised. "I can't pretend any longer that I don't know the right thing to do. Legal ownership has nothing to do with it."

Chapter 9

Celia thudded her way through the small door of the bookstore, grateful for the guitar's hard case. She didn't want any more time to think about this. The guitar would go to its real home as soon as her shift ended.

"I didn't know you played," Melanie said, stepping from behind the counter to help her with the bulky case. "Why are you bringing it in today? You going to come with me to the open mic night I told you about? The trouble is it's only on Thursday."

A laugh burst from Celia as she remembered her short-lived plan to perform as a way to connect with her neighborhood.

"I have a shaky grasp on three chords," she told her coworker. "Even if I knew a song, I certainly wouldn't inflict it on innocent ears."

Melanie shook her head and grinned. "Whatever gave you the idea any ears would be innocent?" Then she raised her hands and backed away from Celia's pretend glare. "Alright. No performances for you. I get it. So why the guitar?"

Celia held the case against her chest as she made her way through the shelves to the employee-only area. All she needed to round out a rough morning was to knock a shelf over. The whole shop would go down like a dominoes display.

Melanie followed, no customers available to distract her. "Come on. If you can't tell me, who can you tell? Do you really want me to expire out of curiosity? Just think of the mess you'd have to deal with. And the police…" She pretended to swoon.

This time, Celia's laugh came out strong and true. "Melanie, what would I do without your antics?"

"You'd settle into morbid dullness, of course. So give."

After setting the guitar out of the way, Celia let out a short sigh. She tucked a loose strand of hair behind her ear and turned to face Melanie.

"I bought it down at Mr. Peterson's Buy-Sell-Trade."

"From that old man? I don't think he likes me. Gives me the creeps the way he shakes his head when I walk by."

Celia smiled, imagining Mr. Peterson found Melanie's designed-to-shock clothing and multi-pierced ears equally as creepy. "He's a nice guy. A real old-world gentleman. You're just a bit more than he can handle, I suspect."

Melanie smoothed a hand down her hair and paused to pull some out of her hoop earrings. "I don't know why. It's not like I have a pierced belly-button or anything."

Pushing down the sudden need to look at the inch of skin exposed between Melanie's short skirt and top, Celia waved aside the concept in favor of telling her story. Now that she'd started, she felt as if she needed to get it out.

"So, the other day he called me in and told me the boy who put the guitar up for sale got in trouble over it. The dad really wants it back."

"Figures." Melanie nodded. "My parents got all over me when I stopped playing the flute. It was all about how much the instrument cost and how I'd never amount to anything. As if blowing my spit around the room would have gotten me anywhere either." She paused to brush the curls from her face. "Yeah, I was really awful. You think you shouldn't perform? You should have heard me."

"Anyway," Celia said, unable to keep the laughter out of her voice at the picture, "Mr. Peterson gave me their address. He said they'd pay me what I spent on the guitar if they could only get it back. Unlike your flute, apparently it's this guitar that's important, not just the concept."

Melanie put a hand on Celia's arm. "And you're going to fall for that? You're going over to a stranger's house to give up something you bought fair and square? If it was so important to the dad, he should have kept better control of it. Don't be a pushover."

Celia couldn't stop her glance toward the case or her sigh. "I tried to think that way, Melanie, I really did. But the only claim I have on this guitar is the money I paid, and he's willing to reimburse me."

She stifled the desire to explain about soul. If anyone would understand, Melanie would, but she didn't want to come off as unbalanced. "I just can't stop thinking about the boy. From what Mr. Peterson said, I don't think he did this on purpose to upset his dad. Caring parents are few and far between. I'd hate to be the cause of a rift growing."

Melanie shook her head. "I believe you're over-thinking this. Sure, parents can get pretty ticked off at their kids, but they get over it. Probably by the time you show up on their doorstep, the dad will have forgotten the fuss, and you'll just embarrass him and the kid both."

The doorbell chimed before Celia could respond, a rescue she gratefully accepted. "I'll get it." She didn't know how to answer the other girl. How could she explain parents like Melanie described were rare and precious? Better the embarrassment than chance something that could fester between the boy and his dad.

Her conviction only grew as mothers brought flocks of little kids in for summer reading, teenagers came for the graphic novels, and a grandmotherly lady arrived to get a present for her niece. Family was important here. Celia wasn't going to let her selfishness stand in the way of getting the guitar back where it belonged.

Melanie laughed at her the third time she went to check on the guitar, but a weird feeling something would go hideously wrong kept plaguing Celia. She'd threaded the address through the strings before leaving her cottage in the morning, and first she thought it had vanished, but no, the small piece of paper remained where she'd put it. Then she heard a weird noise and thought a string had broken. It was only some books she'd set aside to wait for the publication date. She hadn't stacked them securely and the top book threatened to fall. Celia fixed the problem as soon as she realized the cause.

"Maybe you're right." Melanie tapped a pencil on the counter. "You are getting all neurotic about this. Getting it off your hands may be necessary for your sanity."

Though Celia laughed along with Melanie, after that she forced down her worries. Nothing was going to happen to the guitar here. If anything, she probably just felt nervous about going to a stranger's house uninvited. In that, Melanie was right. It would be embarrassing, if not for the dad, then for her. But it was the right thing to do.

BRIAN GLANCED OUT THE WINDOW, surprised to see the growing shadows. He wiped a hand across his forehead, only remembering the paintbrush in his hand when the wet liquid splashed his cheek.

"Damn," he muttered under his breath.

He hadn't forgotten his plan to get out more, but he had to get at least one public room finished. What would he do if Nick invited someone home?

Brian grimaced. He'd seen Nick's sour expression often enough when he tried to talk to his son about the house. Nick wouldn't invite anyone here with it looking like a disaster zone.

The brush dropped onto the paint tray, and Brian stood up, stretching his back.

He'd chosen a light cream, a neutral color and one he could easily paint over if Nick ever showed any interest in how their house looked.

Neutral. That's what they needed. To find some neutral ground.

Neither had mentioned the incident in Nick's room. Brian couldn't figure out a good way to bring it up, and Nick's bad mood hadn't improved. If anything, his son seemed more distant, more on edge, than before. He didn't even want to go down to the park.

Brian went through the cleanup mechanically, his thoughts trapped in the problem of Nick. He hadn't expected to become a father again, and certainly not of his own half-grown son, but he planned to make the best of it—if they survived this. Just thinking about Nick brought a smile, and he savored the happiness despite everything. It kept him from losing his temper so completely that he said something unforgivable.

He'd never realized just how hard childrearing was. He'd found it easy to frown at parents who bribed or yelled at their kids in the grocery store, at those who swatted heads or bottoms. He'd had no idea the pressure they were under.

The rush of water quieted into a distant hiccup when he turned the tap off. Another thing to look at, but for plumbing, he'd call in a professional. Brian stared at his water-slicked expression in the mirror, searching for paint splashes.

Had he always looked so old? His fans hadn't thought so, but they rarely saw him without the stage makeup. Or maybe Kaitlin's death and getting Nick had worn him out more than he'd allowed himself to realize.

A grin split the image, and the exhaustion reflected there melted away.

Maybe he just felt old because he hadn't spent time with a young kid before. Brian couldn't wait until he could blame his first gray hair on Nick. They would laugh together then go play some basketball or something.

Reenergized at the thought, and the realization it couldn't always be this rough, Brian dried off and headed for the kitchen. He had a list of Nick's favorite meals thanks to a quick call to Kaitlin's sister. She'd been an ally in the early troubles between him and Kaitlin, and now seemed willing to help with Nick. She'd never approved of her sister's decision to keep him away.

Irene had offered to take Nick in and raise him with her three so Brian wouldn't be faced with figuring out parenthood this late in the process, but Brian had wanted his son more than anything else. He thought the decision impressed Irene, but he hadn't been out to win any awards. He just wanted to know Nick, to raise the boy. This little guy could be the only significant mark he left on this earth, though he'd had fans a plenty, and he wanted to make the most of it.

"Hey, Nick. Come on down and set the table," he called a little while later. He had a pot of water heating on the stove and a bottle of sauce. Kaitlin probably made it fresh, but she'd never given him much of a chance to be domestic. His mom hadn't believed in guys cooking unless they were fancy chefs or something, so he never developed the knack.

The sound of thumping footsteps warned Brian even before his son stomped into the room.

"What's for dinner?"

Brian pasted a smile on his face, determined to ignore Nick's bad mood until it passed, though it had better do so sooner rather than later. They were going on the second day of this treatment.

"Pasta. With red sauce. Aunt Irene says it's your favorite."

"Well she's wrong!"

The shout startled Brian, and he bumped the pot. Water hissed when it hit the flames, the noise cutting into the silence.

Even Nick looked shocked.

But it didn't last. The boy glowered at Brian, sandy eyebrows gathering above his nose. "I don't want any more pasta. I don't want any more pizza. I don't want any of this."

Brian opened his mouth to say something, but then shut it, unable to think of a single word. Maybe Nick just needed to get this out of his system.

His son slammed a handful of cutlery onto the table, making Brian grateful he hadn't picked up the plates first. "I hate it here. I don't want to be here. I want to be home with my friends. I hate you. You're an awful dad. I wish you'd left me with Aunt Irene. I wish you'd just leave."

Brian found his hand closing around Nick's arm before he'd consciously moved. He kept his grip loose by force of effort. He hadn't known Nick was aware of Irene's offer until now.

"You don't mean that," Brian said, trying to keep his tone even. "We've had some bumps, but we'll get along fine. I know we will."

Nick jerked free. "You just don't get it, do you? I don't want to get along fine. I don't want to be here. And I don't want you. Just go already. You know you will. Just do it. Get your stuff and go. I know Aunt Irene's number. You don't have to worry about me. Don't give me another thought. Just go!"

Brian rocked back from the force of Nick's hands shoving his chest, but the boy's words struck him much harder. He dragged in a breath, his chest tight. Did Nick really mean it? Did Nick really want him to go?

He tried to catch his son's gaze, but Nick turned away and stomped over to the cabinet where the plates were.

"Wait," Brian called, not wanting to see what Nick would do to the dishes.

Tension trembled in the boy's thin shoulders and both fists were clenched tight at his sides. If only Brian could see his face. Then he'd know how much was anger…and how much grief.

Doubts washed over him. Had he been wrong to take Nick? Had it been fair to take the boy away from everything he'd known so soon after losing his mother? Should Brian have let Irene keep him after all? Was he just being selfish?

"Look," he said, pushing a hand through his hair. "I know I'm making mistakes. This is new to me. But that doesn't mean I'm not trying." He willed Nick to turn, but his son just stared at the cabinet.

"Well maybe you should just give up."

Anger. Nick didn't turn away because of tears in his eyes. No, all the boy held was anger.

Something crushed inside Brian. He'd thought they'd connected, thought they were getting better, but maybe it was all
just wishful thinking. What did he know about raising a child?

The deep tones of the doorbell made both of them jerk, as
if the tension between them had grown so tight the rest of the
world had ceased to exist.

Nick almost ran for the door.

"I'll get it," he called over his shoulder. "Probably just more
junk for this broken house."

Brian slumped against the pantry cabinets, unsure whether
to be grateful for the interruption or not. The angst spilling
from Nick's mouth burned. But how much of it held truth?
How could he figure it out if they couldn't talk about anything?
Or maybe he should have been able to know on his
own…maybe if he was any sort of a father.

His gaze slipped to the water, the hated pasta. It had seemed
like Nick yelled forever, but the water still hadn't boiled. Part of
him wanted to throw it out and make something else, but what?
It seemed as though everything he tried only made Nick angrier.

"Some favorite," he muttered, back tense as he waited for
Nick to return. What was taking his son so long?

Chapter 10

Celia shifted the guitar case from her left to right hand, and wondered if she should just turn around and leave. She knew they were home. Raised voices had filtered through the door when she came up the steps. She should have turned away then.

The guitar's weight kept her there.

What had she interrupted? What if they were arguing about the guitar? Could she really pretend not to be involved? Could she just walk away? Or would she always wonder if somewhere a miserable boy kept getting dark looks from his father because she hadn't been generous enough to accept he'd made a mistake.

The memory of Nick's face in the park haunted her, forced her to stay on the doorstep as much as she wanted to leave. She already knew one unhappy kid, and that was one too many.

Celia put the guitar case down and rubbed her aching arm. She couldn't go anyway. She'd rung the bell. It was too late to change her mind.

As if to echo her thought, the door swung open.

Celia glanced up, then down when no adult face appeared. She took a step back and blinked, sure her guilty mind played tricks on her.

"You!"

Nick seemed just as surprised to see her, and why wouldn't he be? She'd never seriously imagined he was the boy Mr. Peterson had told her about.

The shock melted from his expression, leaving a belligerent look in its place. "What are you doing here? I told you not to come. Did you follow me? How do you know where I live? I want you to go away. I don't want to see you ever again, you hear me?"

His reaction might have seemed out of proportion, but she could understand how it looked. She watched in amazement as the door started to close again, too stunned to react. She felt as though she'd stumbled into the middle of a play, only she didn't have the script.

"Hey, wait," Celia managed before the door closed completely, but Nick didn't listen. The latch clicked into place, and she slumped both shoulders.

How could she give up? She didn't just imagine the kid who suffered his father's disapproval. She'd talked to Nick, played checkers. She couldn't walk away now.

A sigh pushed past her lips, and she stuck her finger on the doorbell again. Somehow, she had to convince Nick to listen though she had no idea how she'd manage it, especially since she'd accused his father of abuse the last time they spoke.

BRIAN WANDERED OUT INTO THE hall when Nick didn't return immediately. If it wasn't a package, whoever had come would need to speak to an adult.

Then, he heard Nick yell at the poor person.

The innocent visitor got an earful from what he could hear, and none of it deserved. Nick had just continued their argument, spilling it over on someone unconnected to either of them. They didn't know anyone here.

"You can't talk to people that way," Brian said as he reached his son's side just moments after the door clicked shut. He'd wanted to give a firm, parental warning, but even he could hear the stunned disbelief in his tone.

"She deserved it," Nick muttered, turning away.

Brian grabbed Nick's arm and pulled him back to the door. "Oh no you don't. Whoever she is, she deserves an apology. And you're going to give it to her right now."

He closed his fingers around the handle at the same moment as the doorbell chimed again.

A wry grin pulled at his lips. Nick hadn't cowed whoever it was. Maybe he should feel grateful for Nick's attempt to get rid of the persistent saleswoman.

All humor, all thought, vanished from his mind the moment he pulled the door open.

"What are you doing here?" he demanded, no more polite than his son had been. Whatever he'd expected, to be faced with the woman who had been watching Nick a few nights ago at the park hadn't been on his mind. Was she stalking Nick?

IT'S HIM. THE THOUGHT FLOODED her mind, recognition instant.

As much as she'd tried to dismiss this man, the derelict had never been quite as far from her thoughts as she would have hoped. She stared for a long moment, hearing his question as a distant murmur, unable to understand the words. Then pieces clicked together, and her training reasserted itself. He'd been at the park to drag Nick back to this house, one the boy was too embarrassed of to let her walk him home.

Though she knew an abuser didn't appear different from any other person, she could see this hulking, untidy man swatting Nick hard enough to leave bruises on the boy's slender form whatever Nick had said. As much as her hormones lit up around the man, he'd been the reason Nick had run to the park, and the reason Nick didn't want her here now.

Was the boy afraid for her?

Celia reached for the guitar case and raised it as a shield. She would find out for herself how the boy was living and if he was safe, no matter what stood in her way. She knew the shelter numbers, had looked them up when she first arrived. She could bring Nick to where he'd be safe and this man couldn't find him.

Both Nick and the man fell back at the sight of the guitar, a matching confusion on their faces. Despite the different appearances, she would have known them for father and son instantly.

The hard case held like a battering ram, Celia took advantage of their shock to move forward, pushing her way into a house as bare as the man had been untidy. She caught a hint of fresh paint and wondered what the man had been trying to cover up.

Her fingers tightened on the hard, black case for a moment as she considered whether Nick had sold off their only form of income. No wonder his father was angry. She hadn't seen any street musicians in town, but that didn't mean they weren't there.

Her flash of sympathy faded as quickly as it had come.

Whatever the reason, whatever the consequences of the boy's mistake, no father should make his son so miserable. She planned to give him a piece of her mind if nothing else. And if she saw any sign of real abuse, mental or physical, she'd have Nick out of there faster than the man could blink.

Chapter 11

Brian stared in shock as the woman battled her way through the door and into his house. Who did she think she was?

He knew he should call the police, but instead, he chased after her as she peered into each room. He could handle one woman, no matter how aggressive.

Or so he thought until her hand closed on the one door he'd kept shut since taking over this relic. "No! Not in there."

His cry came too late.

She turned the handle and pulled open the door, releasing the strong stench of urine. Whether dog or person, Brian hadn't cared. He planned to tackle the disgusting job when he had more confidence in his abilities.

She turned back to stare at him, the open door still releasing the smell.

A twinge of embarrassment made him wonder if this was how Nick felt about the whole house. He marched past her to close the door so he could breathe freely, a grimace tugging at his cheeks.

"I told you not to go in there," he said, hearing the belligerence in his voice. He didn't add she'd gotten what she deserved, but he figured it showed on his face anyway.

The woman's eyebrows pinched together, something more than disgust reflected in her expression. "Is this any way to bring up a boy, to bring up your son?"

The question hit with almost a physical force and sent Brian rocking back on his heels. All sorts of explanations clogged his throat, but anger kept them bound.

"What business is it of yours?" he demanded, grabbing her arm roughly and tugging her toward the door.

She tripped, and what she'd been holding in the other arm, the battering ram, dropped from her grasp.

A discordant cry sounded in the hall, and Brian froze, memory crashing down on him.

He stared at the woman, then let his gaze travel to her side and the object she'd been holding.

A guitar case, and not just any case. He knew the instrument's voice as well as his own.

Ignoring the woman, he ducked to her side and reached for the clasps, his hands knowing where to go without needing direction. He had to check if the guitar had been damaged.

Brian shot an angry look at the woman, but kept hold of his tongue when he saw how upset she was.

She hadn't meant to drop it. If anything, he should bear the blame for startling her, but then she wouldn't have been so if she hadn't barged into his home unasked.

The latches flipped one after another, the sharp clack of metal filling the hall. Then he lifted the lid and a sigh rushed out from between his lips.

His guitar. Lullaby Lady.

She lay nestled in the case just as ready for a gig as she'd ever been.

Brian lifted her, running his hands along her body and neck to make sure she'd come to no harm in the fall. She settled onto his bent knee and pulled snug against his frame, happy to be home. He'd been a fool to give her to Nick. He'd just wanted to share something of himself, and music was all he had. But how could a kid understand this?

He pushed away the knowledge he'd been Nick's age when he'd first set fingers to strings. As if to echo his thought, his hand wrapped around her neck, and Brian plucked one string after the other.

The notes rang out discordant, like the cry when she fell, but the sounds held no buzzing or distortion. She was fine. Out of tune, but otherwise unharmed.

Relief filled Brian out of proportion to the event, but a true emotion. He hadn't known how much the guitar had meant to him until losing her. Or maybe not until now, with her in his arms.

"Give her money back, Nick," he called without looking up. "That's what she's here for."

"But we need the money."

Brian's fingers stilled on the pegs he'd started turning unconsciously to tune Lullaby Lady. His gut clenched, and he froze, not knowing what to do. Nick hadn't said he needed the money. He'd said *we*. He still thought Brian couldn't afford to take care of them both.

"You don't have to— It's alright…"

Brian lowered Lullaby Lady into the case and closed the latches one at a time, the firm, crisp sound providing an outlet for his sudden anger.

He pushed the case away from the woman and growled, "Give her the money. We don't need anyone's charity."

He'd have to explain things to his son. He'd tried before, but obviously, it hadn't sunk in. They didn't need any money. They were quite well off. But damn if he was going to tell this woman that, this prejudging busybody who couldn't keep her nose out of his business.

CELIA SHUDDERED AT THE SUPPRESSED violence in the man's tone. No wonder the boy was afraid of his dad.

"Go get it," the man told Nick again.

The boy stood his ground and shook his head. She wanted to grab hold of him and tell him not to taunt the monster, to take the safe route.

Their family crisis was none of her business. She'd moved here to get as far away from situations like these as she could.

Even now, she could feel her heartbeat accelerating and a cold sweat broke out on her palms. She needed to leave, to calm down away from all this. It wasn't her responsibility; it wasn't her job any more.

Celia straightened her shoulders, surreptitiously wiped both hands down the sides of her pants, and stepped forward until she partially blocked their view of each other.

A sharp pinch started in her temples, the beginnings of a headache, but she couldn't walk away. She was part of this whether she wanted to be or not, and it wasn't just the guitar that had drawn her in. She felt more of a connection to this boy than anyone else in the whole town. She couldn't just abandon him.

"Maybe you could keep the money as payment for lessons. On the guitar I mean."

It wasn't much of an answer, but it was all she could come up with to diffuse the situation. She could find another guitar, and Nick could meet her in the park. Maybe someday she'd be good enough for that quality of instrument, but she certainly wasn't now.

Nick stared at her for a moment with wide-open eyes until she was sure he'd reject her plan. Then he nodded so intently she just had to smile.

"That's a great idea," he said, excitement filling his tone. "My dad can teach both of us. He's really good, you know."

Celia's smile drained away and her pulse accelerated even more. Dizziness swept over her. She put a hand to her suddenly damp forehead. Celia couldn't imagine surviving his teaching. Nick's dad made her nervous, unsettled, just being in the same room.

Her mind brought up pictures she tried to find revolting, of him leaning over her, his warm breath on her cheek, his arms wrapped around her as he positioned her fingers. She opened her mouth to protest, to reject the plan, but he spoke first.

"Look, if it would make both of you happy, I guess I could."

She glanced at him, expecting annoyance or aggravation, anything but the almost desperate affection showing on his face as he looked at Nick.

The boy seemed oblivious.

Had Nick shown any interest in the guitar before, something so obviously precious to his dad? Somehow, from the man's reaction, she doubted it. She could not deny them this chance to connect. To become a proper family without all the anger she'd heard in the father's voice.

Celia laughed, the sound startling all of them, even her.

"I'm afraid this has gotten a little tangled," she said and thrust a hand toward the father. "Hi. I'm Celia Baker. I met your son at the park and apparently bought your guitar."

She waited a moment, long enough she thought he would reject her overture, but how could he give her lessons if he wouldn't even give her his name?

A smile pulled at the man's lips, transforming his rough features into pure masculine beauty.

Celia stared, the tension in her chest having nothing to do with her heart or panic, though it felt as if every nerve was involved.

"I'm Brian Lakes."

His lips tightened, the faint smile vanishing as he stared at her.

Celia didn't understand his reaction, but maybe he was just a little off. His emotions sure seemed out of control if this snippet of his life was anything to go by. Setting a good example, she curled her lips in a full smile.

"Nice to meet you." The words came out soft, gentle, almost wistful, but she didn't regret them.

He hesitated a heartbeat more, then long, tapered fingers closed around hers and the warmth of his palm sank into her skin. "Nice to meet you, too."

Maybe her tone had affected him in some small way after all. She thought she detected something a bit wistful in his voice as well.

"Does this mean we can still play checkers in the park?"

Celia pulled her hand free, missing the warmth as soon as Brian let go. She turned to face Nick and bent to match his height. "I'd like that. I'd miss playing if we didn't. I'm sorry I made you angry last time."

His grin in return was the best reward she could have gotten. This kid sure didn't hold grudges.

Celia pushed aside the disturbing feelings she'd had around his dad and reached out to ruffle Nick's hair.

He ducked.

"Why does everyone do that?" he demanded, but she thought she detected a hint of pleasure in the complaint.

Celia glanced toward Brian, and they shared a rueful look before she turned back to Nick. "I guess because your hair is so mussable."

Nick stared at his feet, a red tinge creeping up his neck.

She'd never felt so in tune as in that moment. She wanted it to last forever.

Instead, Celia let a small sigh escape her lips and turned to Brian. "I've intruded long enough. I should be getting home." A home that seemed so empty in comparison for all it had no foul rooms behind closed doors.

Brian walked her to the front entrance, so close her skin tingled with awareness.

He dropped a hand on her shoulder. "When do you want your first lesson?"

Celia turned to stare at him, dumbfounded for a moment before her mind caught up with all that had happened. "When are you available?"

He shrugged. "Whenever. Just tell me so I have time to get cleaned up."

The thought that he needed advanced warning to prepare disturbed her, but at the same time, she couldn't help being relieved. Her fantasies of his lessons never included the ammonia reek of piss, or choking clouds of dust.

At the same time, she thought Nick had been right.

If Brian was here all the time, if he had to plan ahead to make himself acceptable, he obviously wasn't working.

Maybe they did need the money despite how Nick's father had denied it. She'd see how the first one went then figure out how much she could afford per lesson. That way, at least they'd have some money coming in.

"How about Friday? After work—my job. I get off at three. I can be here by three-thirty. Does that suit you?" She held herself still, half hoping he'd say no, that he had a job to go to, that he wouldn't be there until later.

Brian shrugged. "It's fine. You can play Lullaby Lady for now. You don't have to rush out and buy another guitar, though you should so you can practice at home."

Celia nodded and turned to the door. He sounded so normal, so put together, but she'd seen the rest with her own eyes. He clearly wasn't working, and she wondered why. Jobs weren't easy to come by in Foster's Way, but there were jobs here. If he just made an effort.

"Bye, Nick," she called at the last moment. "See you Friday."

Brian gave her a mock salute and closed the door with her on the outside.

She stood there for a few moments, trying to understand everything that had just happened and failing. Finally, Celia shrugged and turned away, heading back to her cottage.

The contradictions in the man were overwhelming, but she didn't have to resolve them now or ever. She only had to take lessons and pay enough for them so Nick could get solid meals. Someone probably gave them the place rent free. She couldn't see how they could afford it otherwise. Maybe Brian had hit rock bottom at some point and was cleaning up his act for his son. Maybe he just needed some time to get settled, to find his feet.

Chapter 12

know there are not enough women authors in our great litera-
ture section, but do you really think Anne Rice qualifies?"

Celia jerked, startled out of her thoughts by Melanie's laughing words. She glanced up at Melanie then down to see the
Anne Rice novel in her hand. Even worse, she'd carefully filed
three other of the vampire books in the same row as Plato. She
sighed and tugged the others off the shelf.

Melanie pulled one of the stepstools over and squatted on it,
her feet wrapped around the wood frame in awkward angles.
"If you were one of my girlfriends, I'd tell you to spill. What's
got you all bound up these past few days?"

A blush heated Celia's cheeks. Shouldn't she have more control over her emotions than a bunch of twenty somethings?

"It has to do with the guitar, doesn't it? That's when you
started acting this way."

Celia stared at her coworker, surprised at Melanie's agile
mind though she shouldn't have been. She half shook her head,
not wanting to talk about it, then stopped. She'd never really
had anyone to confide in before, but never felt the lack until
now.

"Can you be attracted to someone who's the opposite of
everything you want?" She hadn't meant to ask the question, but
it had bothered her ever since she'd agreed to the guitar lesson.
If she closed her eyes even now, she could almost feel the
warmth of Brian's skin against hers, his fingers brushing her
palm.

Melanie laughed. "Of course you can. Don't you ever watch
romantic comedies? Even going back to Shakespeare and *The*

Taming of the Shrew. It doesn't matter what you look like on the outside, what life you lead. Attraction is all about finding someone who sees the real you."

This time Celia did stare at the younger woman.

"Hey, I've worked here since I was fourteen. You think none of this has sunk in?"

Celia shook her head and laughed at the same time. "I guess you're right. Opposites attract and all that." She turned to the restocking box at her side, this time choosing Nietzsche instead of Anne Rice.

"Oh no, you don't. You're not going to leave me hanging. I can spout platitudes all day, and you'll have to listen. The only way to stop me is to tell me what's going on."

"It's complicated."

"When isn't it?" Melanie scooted closer, the stool almost bumping against Celia's folded knee. "That's what makes it so interesting." She grinned and waved Celia to continue.

"You're right that it started with the guitar. I returned it, but the boy didn't want to give the money back. His dad was getting angry, so I suggested lessons. I meant with Nick—did I tell you he's the boy who's been crushing me at checkers in the park?—but he said his dad will teach me."

Melanie shook her head. "It doesn't sound so bad. You like the boy from what you've said about meeting in the park. And if he sold the guitar, pretty much even that he doesn't know how to play. Sounds like you made a decent deal Miss 'I'm shaky on the three chords I know.' So what's the problem?"

Celia jammed another book onto the shelf to avoid Melanie's penetrating gaze, then pulled it out again. "Not mysteries either," she muttered, trying for a laugh.

Shoving the box out of Celia's reach with one foot, Melanie said, "Come on. You can't stop there. What about his dad? Somehow I can't imagine you acting like this over a kid."

Celia twisted her hands together and sighed. "That's the problem. From what I've seen of him, he's some kind of derelict. Probably an ex-druggie or something. And he has a short temper. He's what I'd classify a risk at my old job. You take in the ones that show signs of wanting to change, but this guy...well, he wanted advanced warning to clean up for the lesson. I guess he doesn't think it's important to wash every day. The first time I saw him, he was leaking dirt like that Charlie Brown character in the newspaper comics."

A frown pinched Melanie's face. "That doesn't sound right. Foster's Way doesn't really appeal to the panhandling crowds. Why would he be here?"

Celia pushed to her feet. "I'm guessing he was a street musician. Someone must have leant him the place. And they're not going to be happy when they get it back. It smelled like he's been using it for a latrine."

"Eww." Melanie stood as well and grabbed Celia's shoulders. "You're not that hard up, Celia. He sounds like a real tough case. You want a date, I'll get you one. Don't waste time on this guy."

Shrugging off the hold, Celia turned and trailed her finger along the books, pretending to look for more misfiles. "It's not that simple. The man clearly cares for his son. Maybe he just doesn't know any different. Maybe he's trying to change his life for the better. Maybe..."

Melanie shook her head. "Maybe you're not thinking clearly. You've told me enough about why you came here in the first place. Didn't you want to leave all that behind? You're just a simple book clerk here. You don't have to go out and save people. It's not your responsibility. Let him get counseling if he needs it. You don't want that kind of stress, remember?"

Celia tried to remember, but instead she felt his touch on her shoulder, felt the heat radiating from him to warm her inside and out. Even more, she remembered their shared look over Nick's reaction. It made her feel a part of something as never before.

"Oh no, you've got it bad, don't you? It's the whole opposites attract, bad boy syndrome. Forget what I said about romantic comedies. The bad boy only turns good in the movies. This guy's the first male you've spent any time with other than Mr. Peterson since coming here. Tell me if I'm wrong? You've fixated on the first man with any potential."

"Have I?" She didn't really mean to speak the question. Only she could offer an answer. Had she fixated on the first male in her age range? Or was it more than that? She certainly couldn't save him from himself. She'd learned early on no one could make someone else recover and take the next steps in rejoining the human race. So if she didn't want to save him, what did she want?

She didn't need Melanie's laugh to know her face had turned bright red; she could feel the radiating heat.

"Okay, so maybe I am ripe for a relationship," she said, if only to stop the other girl's laughter. "But a single flash of attraction doesn't mean anything. It certainly doesn't mean I have to follow through with it."

Melanie put an arm over Celia's shoulder and steered her toward the front. "Tell you what. You man the counter. If you've got customers, I doubt you'll let your mind drift. I'll work on the restocking. And if you happen to meet a cute guy, all the better. If you're just ripe, any guy will do."

Celia laughed. "Thank you, Dr. Ruth. I'll just sit up here in a puddle of hormones and wait for a more suitable target." As her laughter faded though, she somehow knew no matter how many 'cute guys' came to buy a book today, none of them would offer up the instant attraction she'd felt even when she'd seen Nick's father at his worst.

"HEY, BRIAN?"

Brian looked up from his omelet, his mind still focused on what to do today. He pushed away his planning when he remembered his decision to spend more time with Nick.

"Yeah? You've got something you want to do today?"

His son glanced down at the table for a moment, and Brian wondered if he regretted speaking out. Sure they fought some of the time, but didn't all families? They could still talk.

"What is it?" Brian asked, careful to keep his voice soft.

Nick fiddled with his fork for a moment longer, then looked up. "You know the lady's coming for her lesson this afternoon."

Brian nodded, Celia's image rising up in his mind's eye without a deliberate thought. Part of him saw her as a complication, but the rest looked forward to her visit.

"Do you think we could do something about that room?"

Surprised, Brian stared at Nick for a few seconds before smiling when he heard the *we* in Nick's statement. "It'll be tough work," he cautioned.

Nick's head sunk down again. "Okay. I'm sure you had something else planned. I just thought—"

"Hold on, now. I wasn't saying no. Just stating the facts. I don't know if we have enough time to make it decent, but we can get started. At least it will be less embarrassing."

They exchanged a rare look of complete agreement.

Nick gave him a smile. "Did you see her expression?" he asked, his tone a mix of embarrassment and laughter.

Brian released his own chuckle, hearing the edge in it. "She thought we were some kind of bums, I'd guess. I could see her heading for disaster, but couldn't move fast enough to stop her. I'd have done anything to keep the door closed."

Nick shook his head. "She sure was pushy. She's not like that at the park...well, not most of the time."

Wondering what had happened between the two of them, it took almost all of Brian's energy to let Nick have his secrets. He pointed at Nick's plate instead of demanding to know how long his son had spent with a complete stranger.

"You'll need every bite of energy you can get. There's a reason I've left the dining room for last. I can't imagine my expression is any more welcoming when the door opens."

Nick screwed his face up into a disgusted look, but his eyes were laughing above it.

"Don't worry. I've got a spare paint mask."

Though Nick chuckled at the last, soon silence fell again, and Brian missed the connection between them. It reminded him of the good times with his own father, before he'd been discovered.

"You know, I used to help my dad with projects sometimes. When I was still at home."

Nick glanced up. "Grandpa told me."

Anger whipped through Brian out of nowhere. Of course his dad told Nick. Kaitlin hadn't barred his parents from seeing their grandson. Only him. How she explained it, he didn't know. He hadn't asked.

"Is that why you're doing this?"

Nick's question pulled Brian back from a bad place, and he looked around the kitchen, one of the first rooms he'd cleaned up. "I don't know. I didn't think about it that way, but maybe. Your grandfather wanted me to become a carpenter just like him. He got me hired on with his contractor crew during the summers and taught me everything he could."

"But you didn't like it?"

Brian laughed aloud. "Would I have taken on this abandoned house if I didn't?" He shook his head before Nick could answer. "I liked it fine, but music called to me so much stronger. Dad tried to be supportive, but I don't think he ever understood."

He'd supported Kaitlin, in fact, believing less of Brian for not staying and making a home for his son. Maybe his father's disapproval had driven Brian to want to show he could after all.

"So we really don't need the money?"

Brian lowered his fork and twisted to face Nick fully. He wanted to reach out, to grab a hand, but didn't know how Nick would feel about the contact. "No. We don't need the money. We're not living in a dump, for all it might have looked like one when we moved in. When I checked out houses, this beautiful Victorian stood out as the one with the most character."

Nick's eyebrows rose, and his eyes danced below them. "Beautiful?"

Whether the boy laughed at his wording or the state of the house, Brian chose to interpret it as the latter. "It has strong bones, as my father would say."

Nostalgia crept over him for the times when he'd helped his dad remodel homes people had neglected. If he could give Nick even a fraction of the memories his dad had given him, Brian would consider this house a success no matter how it turned out. He'd thought that impossible with Nick refusing to help, but maybe things were changing. This was the first time they'd talked so long without arguing.

Brian didn't know what his son's thoughts held as they finished their breakfast in silence, but his slid from his father's rejection of his career to dwelling on Celia Baker, a much more pleasant topic. What was her story? She had to have one. She certainly didn't act the way most women did around him.

Brian laughed at himself as he pushed away from the table and grabbed his plate. Did he think her unusual because she hadn't even reacted to his name? Because she didn't want his autograph or an invite into his room? Maybe he'd been out of the real world for too long to recognize normal when it stood right in front of him.

The warm water splashed over his hands, but his mind wasn't on the dishes even when Nick added his to the pile and took up the drying towel. They'd established this pattern because they had only enough dishes for each meal, something else he'd failed to manage properly.

What business did he have pretending he knew how to live a normal life? He'd been in the music scene since before he'd even graduated high school, though only locally. He knew the life, was comfortable there. Everything he did now seemed awkward, as if he pretended to be someone he wasn't.

"You missed a spot."

Brian turned to see Nick's grin as the boy pointed out a piece of egg still attached to the plate he'd passed along.

"Hmm," he said. "You better give me the plate, then." He let a smile stretch his own cheeks, accepting Nick's delight at being able to catch him out.

Yes, this life might be new to him, but he'd adapted before. Just seeing Nick's happiness made it worth every sacrifice he'd made. The music world could wait. Nick needed him now.

For all his fumbles, if he looked back on the solemn boy he'd picked up a week after Kaitlin's funeral, he could see the difference. Nick had his quiet moments, and they'd certainly had clashes, but they'd come a long way. Maybe the house would help them finally become a true family.

He might not have admitted how much the thought of working side by side with Nick had influenced the choice of this house, but the extra space it offered had appealed from the start. Music still hummed in the back of his head like an addiction he hadn't really kicked, but this time he'd do it right.

He'd wait for Nick to grow comfortable here, to recover his confidence, before even thinking about returning to the music scene. Then he'd make over one of the extra bedrooms into a studio so he'd still be home for Nick. No more spending every week on the road. He'd be happy playing the local scene and recording his songs right here. Times had changed, and now a musician had options.

Shaking off dreams of a perfect future, Brian handed the last plate to Nick and twisted the knob to stop the flow of water.

"Come on, Nick. Finish drying the last one and let's get into some grubbies, put on our masks, and get to work. We have a lot to do before your lady friend comes."

"Hey!" Nick slid the plate onto the pile of clean dishes without looking up, but a red flush stained the back of his neck at the tease.

"I'll put these away," Brian offered in apology. "You go get ready."

Watching his son dash out of the room, Brian felt his heart warm. This was what he'd hoped for when he chose a house that needed work. For them to bring it back to glory together, to share the process. And if it had taken the intervention of a beautiful woman, who was he to complain?

She'd done him two favors: returning his guitar and helping his son open up. Brian realized he was looking forward to her visit despite how it would tempt him beyond endurance. She'd been forceful, sure, but the way she'd helped Nick when Brian had tried to push the money issue overrode any annoyance. He looked forward to teaching her how to play, and teaching Nick.

Maybe the music would be another connection with Nick. He'd given his son Lullaby Lady in the hopes Nick would ask to learn, but he didn't know whether he'd done it to strengthen a shaky bond with his son or because he needed the excuse to play. Maybe, instead of giving up his first love, he should have been sharing it all along. And that meant more than shoving a guitar into untrained hands and hoping for the best.

Between the money questions and not understanding the importance of Lullaby Lady, Brian had to wonder if Nick even knew his dad had been at the heart of the country music scene. He'd have thought Kaitlin would have mentioned that much, though maybe she and Brian's father decided it would be a bad idea. His mother wouldn't have fought the decision even if she disagreed. She never contradicted his dad in front of Brian, even when he knew she didn't support his dad's position.

His parents weren't bad people. He loved them both, and he knew they returned the feeling. But they hadn't realized his talents would take him away from normal life, and it still didn't sit well with them.

Brian tucked the dishes into the cabinet and closed the door on them and his sour thoughts at the same time. It didn't matter what Kaitlin had done. She didn't control Nick anymore. Brian refused to let his frustrations with his ex-wife destroy the fragile bond he'd started to create with his son.

CELIA WAVED TO MR. PETERSON as she rushed past, but she didn't waste any time chatting. She'd told him the happy ending to his guitar story earlier in the week and wouldn't have been able to put together a coherent word in any case.

Her heart throbbed, but she knew her pace had nothing to do with it. She'd spent all day trying to pretend she wasn't looking forward to the lesson, and for all the wrong reasons.

Now that she didn't have to put on a face for Melanie and the customers, though, she let her grin through. It was stupid to be anticipating this so much. What did she really know about either of them?

Even if Brian wasn't responsible for the pungent scent in the closed off room, couldn't he have found a better place to raise his kid? And couldn't he take the time to shower every once in a while?

Celia tried to frown as she turned her key in the lock, but even his lack of hygiene couldn't break her eagerness. She shook her head. Was she really that desperate, or was there something about this guy? Maybe her connection with his son caused her reaction.

A laugh burst from her.

She liked Nick—had liked him since she first saw him at the park—but somehow she didn't think she'd spend so much time thinking about the father just for the sake of his son. Or if she had been, the thoughts would focus less on the man's athletic build and the way his voice sent a shiver down her spine.

Her purse clattered against the Formica kitchen table, and she strode past to her bedroom. She'd have to be quick if she wanted to be there on time.

The closet stumped her.

She didn't want to wear work clothes, and if she dressed up just to show them, wouldn't they all be uncomfortable? They lived in a piss-soaked dump. What could she wear that would fit in?

Celia glanced at her watch. If she was going to have time to pick up the take-out pizza she'd ordered before leaving work, she had to get moving. She grabbed a pair of blue jeans and went to her dresser for a t-shirt. Maybe not the most elegant of clothing, but it was clean and unstained. At least in these she wouldn't call attention to their circumstances. She didn't want to make them feel bad.

She jammed the clothes on, swiped her purse on the way out, and almost forgot to lock the front door. Celia laughed at herself as she turned back. In her old life, forgetting something like that would be unthinkable. Here, Mrs. Whitman next door would be sure to tell her if anyone went inside. The lady was insatiably curious and almost desperate for Celia to do something interesting.

Sometimes, Celia felt the same way. But not today. Today, she had plans no matter how strange, and confusing, they might be.

Chapter 13

Brian finished drying himself from the shower, and sniffed his hands and arms just to be sure. He'd told Nick to wash up as well, so they'd fought for the hot water, but at least they didn't need mechanics' soap to get the smell out.

He glanced at the clock, and his chest tightened. She'd be here any minute now, and he hadn't set up the parlor. Brian jammed his legs into a clean pair of jeans and tugged a black t-shirt over his head, the cloth growing damp where it touched his hair. He stared at the spot only to realize a bigger problem.

"Damn." Brian stripped the shirt off again and dug out a different one from his drawer, a shirt without one of his album covers. The fans loved seeing him in his own t-shirts, but he didn't want to think of Celia Baker as a fan—and she'd given him no reason to either.

Brian strode out of the room, down the stairs, and into the parlor. This had been where he'd planned to spend the day. He'd wanted to smooth out the jagged edges, maybe even move some real furniture in here before she came.

Frustration vanished as he grinned. He'd survive plaster-covered floors and folding chairs in return for an afternoon spent with Nick any day.

The thought reminded him, and he leaned out of the room to call up the staircase. "You'd better hurry, Nick. She's coming soon."

No answer echoed down to him, but Brian shrugged. He had things to do that didn't leave time to chase after Nick.

He went back into the parlor and grabbed the broom he'd left in place for today's task. She'd have to understand they were remodeling, but that didn't mean he wanted to choke her with the dust.

Once he'd brought some level of order to the floor, Brian tugged out the folding chairs. He set them up so Nick and Celia would face him, then shifted them into a sort of circle, then considered moving them again.

Brian laughed at his own indecisiveness. Nick had pushed him into this, but he hadn't objected one bit.

Something about the woman intrigued him. She seemed not to react to his presence at all. He wasn't used to that.

Brian ran the fingers of one hand through his damp hair to comb it, but the strands tangled into a hard knot. He pulled his fingers free and tossed the offending hair over one shoulder. He needed to plan some time to cut it, but so many other things were more important.

Like whether or not Celia found him attractive. He laughed aloud at the wayward thought.

Since when had he cared? He'd always had dozens of women available if he wanted female companionship, and sometimes when he didn't. Kaitlin had no reason to worry when they were together, though. Opportunity hadn't appealed until she threw him, and their marriage, away.

Even here, if he set foot in some of the local bars, he'd probably have more offers than he wanted, especially if he were recognized. Why did this one matter so much?

A review of the few times he'd seen her provided an easy answer, and with it, reassurance. He'd been attracted to her from the start, even when all he'd seen was a nice stride heading away from the shop. And if he wasn't mistaken, he wasn't alone in the attraction.

The doorbell rang, four chimes filling the empty room.

He jogged out to the stairs and started up them. "Nick, where are you?"

Hearing the hint of desperation in his tone made Brian see the humor in the situation. He'd never been nervous around women before, a curse as often as a pleasure. This new life of his had to be the cause. It offered a wealth of surprises.

"The day I can't handle a woman is the day I should put a lily on my chest," he muttered. Brian ran down the few steps he'd climbed in search of his son—and a buffer. His bare foot hit the landing just as the bell sounded again, sending up a small puff of plaster.

He glanced down and sighed. His lower legs and damp, bare feet had collected a good bit of the plaster he'd intended for the dustbin. So much for making a better impression.

Brian padded across the unpolished wood floor and pulled the door open only to see the top of her head.

"I dropped the napkins," she muttered, turning away from him to catch fluttering white objects.

Brian bent to help her, but not before his gaze took in how the denim of her jeans hugged nicely rounded thighs. She reached after one napkin trying to escape on the wind, and the cotton t-shirt pulled tight over a small breast that would fill his hand perfectly if he was any judge.

He tried to concentrate on the task instead, jerking his thoughts away from her delicate frame before they manifested in the front of his jeans. A napkin floated past him on its way into the scraggly yard, and Brian grabbed it. His fingers closed on the paper and her hand as well. A tingle raced up his arm before he could pull away.

"Thanks."

He didn't know if wishful thinking made her voice sound breathless, but she showed no interest in pulling free as they stared at each other.

"Pizza!"

Nick's battle cry jerked Brian out of his preoccupation, and he drew in a deep breath. The smell of melted cheese, cooked sausage, and grease filled his senses.

"Pizza," he muttered, stunned he'd missed the large, cardboard box she had balanced on one hand with an expert's skill.

She shrugged. "I thought since this was unexpected, I'd bring something to eat. I know how much growing boys inhale food like it's the end of the world."

Brian stared at her, wondering how she could know something like that. Did she have a bunch of kids waiting at home? If she had a family of her own, he must have mistaken the interest he'd seen. Did she think they were some kind of charity case? First the lessons and now making sure he kept his kid fed?

He opened his mouth to reject the offer, but didn't have the chance.

"I'll take it back to the kitchen," Nick said, ducking around Brian to snag the box out of her hands. "We can eat in there."

She shot Brian a rueful look, and he let his tension go with a sigh.

Maybe she just meant well.

"Umm, we're not going in there, are we?"

At her question, Brian turned to see they'd left the dining room door open, blocking her view of Nick's passage deeper inside.

He strode toward it and closed the door firmly. They'd made good progress stripping the tainted wallpaper and soaking everything with baking soda, but the room was far from done.

"No. That one is definitely not ready."

Her mouth quirked up in a smile, and as much as he didn't want to join in, soon his tilted as well.

"The house still needs a lot of work," he said, waving toward the kitchen.

CELIA FOUGHT AGAINST THE DESIRE to lean into the hand at her back, its warmth seeping into her bones. She'd been thrown off by how he'd answered the door, his bare feet dusted in the layer of dirt that seemed to follow him everywhere. But when she'd looked up and taken in all of him from the wet hair, to clean clothes and a smile, her preconceptions had shuddered.

With his hair swept free of his face, she couldn't miss how stunning he appeared. Maybe not handsome in a traditional sense, but compelling. He'd certainly caught her attention, enough so Celia only now recognized the strain she'd seen when he answered the door.

And why shouldn't he be tense. If he invited her in, she'd see everything he'd tried to hide the last time, everything that pointed out what he had been and could be still.

Curiosity made her fingers itch when he moved her past the now closed door for all she hadn't wanted to have the lesson in there. Part of her wanted to see it, to prove her memory had no grounding in fact. Or maybe she needed the reminder of why any attraction was impossible.

His reaction, and initial tension, seemed to support what she'd seen, something she needed to keep in the front of her mind.

He paused at the door to a nice, if outdated, kitchen. Over his shoulder, she saw Nick tugging dishes from the cabinets. The pizza steamed on the table, its cardboard lid thrown open.

"Oh." Celia put a hand across her mouth to stifle the exclamation a moment too late.

Of course he'd been tense. She had been so caught up in making sure Nick got a good meal, she hadn't thought how his father might take the gesture.

"I hope you don't mind. About the pizza, I mean. I just thought I should bring something…" She trailed off, bitterly aware of how nervous she appeared.

Brian glanced down at her, then at Nick, a frown on his face. "You didn't have to," he muttered, the restored tension showing in his shoulders.

Celia could tell he wished he could refuse the gift, but couldn't find a way. She drew in a breath, determined to defuse the awkward silence.

"Good." She ducked around him to enter the kitchen. "I'm starving, Mr…"

Once again her voice trailed off as she realized she didn't remember his last name. She twisted to glance at him, surprising an amused look.

"I can't very well call you Nick's father to your face, and I'm afraid I've forgotten your name." She allowed a small smile, accepting his humor and keeping her knowledge of his first name to herself.

The silence fell again, this time expectant.

Brian shrugged. "Lakes. Brian Lakes."

He stared at her as though expecting some reaction, just as he'd seemed to the first time he'd told her. Or maybe he just hoped she'd finally remember it.

Celia nodded her acceptance, filing his whole name away for the future. Assuming they allowed her to return for another lesson.

"I'm Celia Baker in case you didn't catch it before either." She saved him from the embarrassment of having to ask. Even as she gave her own name, though, part of her wondered who he'd been before he fell through the cracks. Maybe she would have recognized the name if she'd lived a normal life before this.

Had he been a local politician? A well-known shopkeeper? Some local celebrity anyone else would recognize?

"I know."

She glanced up at him again, surprised to catch him looking at Nick rather than her. But then, she'd introduced herself to his son over checkers what seemed like an age ago, and Nick probably reminded him before the visit. He had no reason to remember her otherwise.

"Right." To distract herself from his deep, almost black eyes, Celia took in the elegant molding and the underlying beauty where before she'd only seen the ancient stove and worn table.

"This is a beautiful room, a beautiful Victorian. It must have been quite elegant once," she said without thinking.

He looked at her for a moment, then nodded without saying a word.

Celia tried not to kick herself as she watched him take a place at the table.

The house might once have been elegant, but now it showed signs of heavy wear, and even some damage if the plaster dust on his feet was any sign. How could a man like him be expected to restore it to its former glory? And how stupid of her to emphasize his inability. She had no right to sit in judgment. Her life had little in common with what one might expect.

BRIAN SANK INTO HIS CHAIR, still puzzling over her lack of reaction first to his face and then his name. He'd never had someone forget meeting him before, not Brian Lakes. He'd been all but a household name when he'd given up the music for Nick.

Celia made some comment and he responded, but he hadn't really been listening. How could she not know him? Had she been living under a rock?

Even if she didn't follow the country music scene, his problems with Kaitlin had made the cover of the supermarket weeklies more than once ten years ago. They'd fought hard to keep Nick's picture out of the papers, but somehow the reporters couldn't find the same compassion for his privacy.

Or did she know and not care?

That didn't seem possible. How could she connect with someone Nick's age and yet be so disconnected with the music of the times? It wasn't like she was some old granny.

Nick thunked two dinner plates onto the country block table and spun the pizza box to face him. He liberated four pieces, dumping them into the cereal bowl he'd brought for himself.

"Put some back," Brian said, then softened his tone with effort. "Celia will think I never feed you."

He reached for a plate, only then realizing how junky the faux china looked, and he didn't even have enough for all of them. He hadn't been thinking of company when he'd discovered these in a cabinet and checked one more chore off his list.

"I meant to get better dishes," Brian said, unsure why he felt the need to explain.

"Oh, they're very…appropriate." She glanced around and her gaze settled on the stove. "They match the stove perfectly. It's just charming."

Brian's elaborate explanation about how the remodeling was taking up all his time melted away as she touched on his new hobby. "The stove is gas, but is one of the first with electric igniters to light the burners. This house was once fully done in gas, and then somewhere along the line, electricity was added. That's about when the stove went in. Some of the walls still have sconces for gas lights."

Chapter 14

They talked about the house for a while, Brian's knowledge surprising her though she supposed he didn't have much else to do. Her quick drop into familiarity, comfort, also surprised her.

Celia smiled, staring at the tabletop but really reviewing the contradictions she'd found in this man. Again, she couldn't help thinking about who and what he had been before he'd sunk low. Somehow, she couldn't imagine someone with his dynamic personality failing at anything.

"I'm going to put a music room into one of the bedrooms—"

The way his voice stopped so abruptly pulled Celia back to the conversation. She glanced up to find him staring at her, waiting for something. It was the same look he'd given her after both times when he'd shared his name. She still didn't know whatever he expected her to do.

Celia scrambled to pick up the threads and said, "Is it to have space to teach Nick?" She hoped the boy could manage a better trade than following in his father's footsteps as a street performer, but music could serve many purposes, she supposed. Nick was quick and smart. Given the right encouragement, he could do anything.

Brian frowned. "Among other things," he muttered.

He took a bite of his pizza, Nick having devoured more than the original pieces he'd claimed while neither of the adults finished their second. "So what kinds of music do you like?"

The direct question caught Celia off guard, and she couldn't come up with an answer. She wasn't used to talking about herself.

Then, she realized it probably had to do with the lesson. Despite appearances, this wasn't a social visit. He must have wanted to know what type of music she was interested in learning.

"You must have a broad repertoire," she said, thinking he'd have to be flexible as a street musician. He could probably teach her any type of music she named. Whatever brought in the most coins.

Brian stared at her for a long moment, another of those odd, expectant looks, then said, "No. Most of my experience is in country."

"Oh. I would have thought..." Celia shook her head to stop the foolish words spilling from her mouth. Why would she want to insult him in his own home?

To repair the situation, she added, "I don't know about around here, but my charges didn't listen much to country. They assigned me rap and rock mostly, to keep me up on the current scene. Some of the other counselors were old folkies though, 60s hippies."

She gave a weak laugh, uncomfortable with revealing even that much of herself. Being too open only left a person vulnerable to hurt where she'd been living.

"You worked with kids?" Brian chuckled, his mouth stretching in a broad, comfortable smile. "No wonder you and Nick get along so well."

She glanced at the boy, who was now downing a tall glass of milk, and almost laughed at the expression on his face. Nick clearly remembered some of the "discussions" they'd had.

"Runaways mostly," she said, then paused, stunned at how willing to talk she seemed to be.

Brian frowned. "That's got to be rough. You're not doing it anymore, are you? I thought Foster's Way..."

"There are runaways everywhere, but no, I'm not working as a counselor here. I-I needed a break." She smiled to cover her discomfort.

A sound rumbled in Brian's chest, maybe a sigh of relief. The look he sent Nick wiped out the last of Celia's concerns. There was nothing but love and worry in his expression. Whatever their circumstances, Brian cared about this boy.

Brian pushed his now-empty plate away and stood up. "Well, we'd better get started. Thanks for the meal."

He shot Nick a significant look that almost made Celia laugh aloud. Nick muttered his thanks and gave her a shy grin.

"Just make sure you wash your hands with soap. None of the pizza grease is getting on Lullaby Lady." Brian took his plate and hers over to the sink, washing both immediately.

Celia sent a questioning look to Nick, but the boy only shrugged.

"Lullaby Lady?" she asked.

Brian glanced over his shoulder, a grin lighting up his expression. "I know, hokey name. But that's what she was when I got her. My Lullaby Lady. She was my very first guitar, and she taught me everything I know."

Celia remembered how the guitar felt, as if it had a soul, a wealth of history. His first guitar, which implied there'd been others afterwards. But how he kept hold of this one through what must have been a difficult transition meant something.

"Sink's free. Scrub up and we'll get started."

Jerked from her thoughts, Celia rose and crossed to the sink. She made sure to use the grease-cutting detergent, determined not to harm a guitar that had to be precious. Now she understood his reaction when she'd dropped the case.

At the same time, Celia realized all their dishes were not only washed, but while she'd been thinking, Nick had dried and put them away. Whatever the story behind the closed room, Brian clearly taught his son proper manners and good habits.

"Good job," Brian said, giving her another smile that wiped out her flash of annoyance at his condescension. He had every right to be possessive of the guitar, and she meant to treat it like the treasure it obviously was.

"Come on, Celia." Nick grabbed hold of her arm and pulled her from the kitchen.

She followed willingly enough until she saw them approach the door she'd opened before. Celia stumbled, but Nick kept urging her forward. How could he expect her to go in there? The "he" in her thoughts was a lot taller than Nick and had shaggy black hair.

At the last moment, Nick swerved across the hall and opened a door on the other side. Celia swallowed her sigh of relief and stepped inside a room almost large enough to hold her whole cottage. She hadn't realized its size the last time, but then she'd only taken a quick glimpse.

"I know it doesn't look like much, but my dad's working on it."

The size of the room had compelled her attention, but Nick's words made her look more closely. There was no permanent furniture in what would normally hold at least a couch and a television. Only three folding chairs, basic plastic ones, stood on the floor. She didn't know whether to be surprised at how little they had, or that they had three chairs, especially considering the lack of dishes. Of course, they could use the third as a makeshift table.

Brian came in right behind them and waved both to sit down. "I guess we can start off with folk. I know some songs from when I first started. It'll be easier if you don't have to think about the song and what your fingers are doing at the same time."

"What?" Celia asked, already laughing. "You're not going to start me out with a rap or rock song?"

"Lady, that's so far out of my area of expertise, I wouldn't know where to start." He topped off the words with a pretend swipe of his cowboy hat.

Celia laughed harder, the plastic chair creaking under her.

"Looks like you're rocking already," Nick cried, his higher laugh adding to hers.

Brian put on a mock fierce look and scowled at them. "Enough fooling around. We're here to learn some music, got it?"

Nick and Celia straightened and nodded together as if they'd practiced the move.

"So, what do you want to do first?" Brian asked.

Celia shook her head, unsure what to suggest.

"Play us something," Nick commanded before she could come up with an answer.

"I'm supposed to be teaching you two. Celia, what do you know already?"

"I have a book Mr. Peterson sold me, and I watched some videos online, but I really don't know anything."

Brian smiled at her. "That's perfect. Nick doesn't know much either, do you, Nick?"

The boy shook his head, then said, "But you should play first. Show us what to do."

Celia watched the exchange between the two, wondering at its intensity.

Hadn't Nick heard his father many times? Or was he just grandstanding, showing off his father's talents to impress her.

"You don't have to," she murmured, putting out a hand to brush Brian's knee. Heat sparked up her arm at the touch, and she drew back, startled.

He looked at her for a moment, as though he'd felt the shock as well, then smiled. "I suppose I could play a little. Just to show you why it's worth the trouble of learning."

Nick practically bounced out of his seat and charged toward the guitar case. "I'll get it out for you."

"Her. Lullaby Lady is a her," Brian said, but Celia could hear the laughter underlying the correction in his tone. "Be careful with her now."

They might have been fighting, shouting loud enough she could hear them through the door, when she'd first visited, but watching them now, they seemed comfortable, happy even. She wondered if they knew how much they cared about each other, how much their love was obvious to an outside observer.

Brian took the guitar from Nick's arms and ran his fingers across the sound hole. He bent closer and adjusted two strings, hearing minute shifts Celia could not. What had taken her hours, and even then only made it close, Brian completed in a matter of minutes without resorting to the pitchfork that had come with the guitar.

"She has a sweet sound. The sweetest of all in the shop where I bought her. That's what's important, not what name's on the label or how much you lay down. The guitar's got to sing."

Celia nodded her head, but her thoughts were far from the purchase of this, or any other, guitar. She watched Brian and Nick work together. It didn't matter if they were the richest people on the block, or dirt poor. What mattered was how they cared. They had no idea how rare what they had was.

Brian's fingers settled into position, adjusting automatically to Lullaby's wider neck compared to the Ovation he'd played on stage. Peace washed over him, and he closed his eyes for a heartbeat, breathing in the dusty, polished wood scent of Lullaby Lady as if he could taste their history together.

He'd been so busy working on the house so Nick wouldn't be ashamed to live here, he hadn't found the time to play the guitar, even now that she was back in his—Nick's—possession. Or had he been avoiding this moment?

Deep down inside, Brian feared what would happen if he played. The moment he allowed music into his life, he didn't know if he'd be able to give it up again.

His eyes slowly opened, and he glanced at the other two. They wore matched, expectant expressions on their faces, anticipating his next move. Had Nick ever heard him play?

He could remember when Nick was just a baby, chortling and gabbling along with him when he practiced at home, but Kaitlin had hated that. She called it a cacophony of sound and told him to rent a practice studio. Her true motive didn't become clear until she forbade him from bringing Nick down with him on the few times he'd been at home.

Was he doing any better? Just like Kaitlin, he'd denied Nick the beauty of music. He didn't even play the radio while he worked on the house, preferring silence to the reminder.

This would have to change. He refused to keep Nick from the music that filled Brian's soul just because he missed it too much. Celia had given him the perfect way to start making amends.

He flashed her a smile, which widened into a grin at her startled reaction. Brian was starting to think her purchase of Lullaby Lady had been a gift, rather than a nightmare.

His knee still tingled where she'd touched it. What was it about this woman?

"Is it that hard?"

Nick's whisper jerked Brian back to awareness and the realization he'd been sitting there, his hands draped over the strings, for some time. He pushed out a laugh and shook his head.

"No. It's not hard at all. Well, once I remember a folk song."

"Do you know *Both Sides Now*?" Celia asked, obviously trying to help.

"They really were hippies, weren't they?" Brian smiled and shifted Lullaby Lady into the right position. "I don't know that one by heart, but here's something older." Brian hummed his way through the first verse to find the right chords to *Danny Boy*, but by the second, Celia's higher voice joined his.

A sense of pleasure washed over him, so different from the adrenalin rush while on stage. She didn't have a perfect voice, and he fumbled the chord placement a couple of times as he tried to figure out another section, but sharing the music soothed him in a way he'd never before experienced.

"Play another," Nick demanded as the last chord hung in the air. "Play another."

Brian dipped his head in an abbreviated bow, feeling this request for an encore warm his heart. "One more, then you two have to get to work."

Celia smiled at him. "You play beautifully," she said.

He wanted to protest, to explain the simple chords he'd used were nothing in comparison to the riffs and fingerpicking he used in performances, but he kept quiet. What was the point anyway? She'd enjoyed his efforts.

He bowed over the strings and played a quick series of notes as he thought, trying to dredge up another folksong. A wry smile tugged at his cheeks when he realized he'd answered, just not in words. But if Celia had never seen a live performance, how would she know the complexity of his noodling.

The next song he thought of, *Waltzing Matilda*, had little in common with the mournful tone of *Danny Boy*, for all it told of a hanging. Soon, Nick joined in on the chorus with enthusiasm even though he didn't know the song. His son had a wonderful voice and showed himself to be a quick study, with every note on key.

Brian couldn't understand why it had taken him so long to discover this connection between them. He vowed to make the most of it from this moment on, starting with a real guitar lesson.

"Okay, Nick, you're up," Brian declared, rising from his chair with Lullaby Lady in his arms.

Nick tensed. "It's her lesson. She should go first."

Brian leaned close and whispered, "Don't you want to show her how it's done? Make her comfortable?"

Nick glanced over at Celia then back to share a conspiratorial grin with Brian before he nodded.

Brian placed the guitar on Nick's knee and positioned the boy's arms then walked around to where he could guide Nick's fingers. Even as he helped his son through the three basic chords, his mind had already leapt ahead to when his arms would be wrapped around Celia, doing the same. Brian shivered, the anticipation wakening rare emotions.

Chapter 15

Celia shifted her fingers again, this time finding the right position despite the distraction of Brian's arm resting along hers.

"That's perfect."

His soft whisper brushed her cheek as he leaned forward to judge her work. If she turned her head just a bit, their lips would meet.

Celia jerked, stunned by her thought. Her fingers dropped away from the neck.

"You'll have to hold them there a bit longer, though, to actually make music. The guitar is a two-handed instrument."

She heard the laughter in his voice and added her own. "I know, I know. Sorry. I guess my fingers are just getting tired."

Though ashamed of the lie, she wouldn't admit the real reason to him no matter what. The ache in her fingers showed some truth to it.

He walked around front and picked up her hand. A tutting sound came from him as he stroked her fingers, his warmth penetrating her sensitive skin.

"I forget how quickly fingertips without calluses get sore." He tapped her palm with his fingers. "You can feel how my calluses have become part of my fingers. It would take years without playing before they went away."

He stepped back, and the distracting strokes stilled.

Celia wondered what went on behind his eyes. What would he have done if she hadn't returned the guitar? Would his calluses have faded, along with whatever dreams he might once have had?

She shivered, missing the warmth of his body pressed against her, of his arms wrapped around her. Laughing inwardly, she tugged her hand free.

"It will take forever for me to build up calluses," Celia said, proud at how she controlled the tremor in her voice. "I'll only be playing once a week when I come here."

Brian lifted Lullaby Lady from Celia's lap and took the two steps to his own chair, but she could tell from his expression his thoughts were distant.

"You're right. We'll have to get you a guitar of your own. If you don't practice, you'll never learn."

Celia pushed down the thought that she wouldn't mind coming here forever. Despite their rocky beginnings, she'd had fun with her lesson, she'd enjoyed talking with Brian before, she loved listening to him play, and his presence made her comfortable in a way she couldn't quite understand.

As if her comfort had pushed over into something else, a yawn stretched her mouth. Celia smothered it and gave a self-conscious laugh, but the dark outside the windows broke her mood.

"It is getting late," Brian murmured. "Later than some can manage."

She almost objected, but then she followed the path of his gaze. At some point, unnoticed by either of them, Nick had slipped off his chair and now lay curled on the floor, fast asleep. With the resilience of youth, the hardwood didn't interfere with his doze, and his arms pillowed his head.

"They're amazing, aren't they?"

Brian's whisper held such awe, Celia turned to stare at him instead. She'd grown up around kids who could do amazing things, but she'd never really thought of it that way. It was always a scramble to get something to eat, to snatch some sleep in a safe place, to survive. She'd never taken the time to realize how amazing it really was.

She smiled, unsure what to say but struck again by how much Brian seemed to care for his son. From the little comments they'd both made at dinner and during the lesson, she now knew Brian had taken Nick in after his mother's death. No wonder they were having a rough time. At least someone had this house to lend them. Otherwise, Nick would have grown up on the street, no different than Celia and her charges.

"Tell you what…"

Brian's words broke through her thoughts, and she turned to find a lopsided smile on his face. "Hmm?"

"I'll play you one more song—an appropriate one, I think—and then walk you home."

She nodded, accepting the song if not the company on the walk. She didn't want to be responsible for Nick waking up alone.

He settled his arms around the guitar, cradling it like a lover, and started playing. As it had many times that night, his singing voice enthralled her. With the right circumstances, he could have ended up on stage, entrancing millions, not in this dump or playing on street corners. His talents were wasted on trying to teach her, but at least now she understood the instrument better.

Then, the words to the song penetrated her thoughts on the music industry's loss, and she laughed aloud before shoving a fist against her mouth to smother the sound so she wouldn't wake Nick. Laughter still shook her shoulders though, and she couldn't remember when she'd felt so relaxed.

The grin on Brian's face as he sang the last chorus stretched almost from ear to ear like a cartoon character. The last note faded and he too burst into laughter.

"What was that song?" Celia demanded in a whisper. "Did you just make it up?"

Brian shook his head. "I wish I had thought of it. It's *Gone Country* by Alan Jackson. I thought it would be appropriate."

She mocked a frown. "You think you can turn me to your country ways?"

He leaned forward to brush a stray strand of hair from her face. "It would be my pleasure."

She stared into his deep brown eyes and read all kinds of meanings into the simple phrase before she forced herself to look away. "Well, you've got a long way to go from tonight's performance. Mine not yours." Celia pretended to yawn, only to have it turn into a genuine one. "But I really should be heading home. I don't think I have anything left for learning more."

Brian rose with her and turned to tuck Lullaby Lady away into her case. "Just remember to practice the fingering. It'll be harder without a guitar to guide your fingers, and it won't give you any calluses, but at least you won't forget what you managed tonight."

"I will. Though I'll close my curtains first so the neighborhood kids don't laugh."

As if one, they turned to look at Nick, still fast asleep on the floor.

"You really should get him to bed. He's exhausted."

"I wish there were more kids around his age here," Brian murmured as if he hadn't heard her at all. "He needs to make some friends, get comfortable."

Celia didn't answer, knowing she had nothing to offer. Even if Nick did meet some kids, he couldn't bring them home to play, not with the chance someone would open the dining room door. And how would he feel when he tried to offer them a snack and didn't have enough plates to go around?

She looked between the two of them and sighed.

Brian had made a tough choice, but it was the right one. Even living like this, Nick would have a better life with one parent to love him than being one among a crowd in the foster care system. No matter how good the foster parents, there were just too many needy kids.

"I could help you—"

"No. He's got to find friends on his own. We'll do okay. It just takes time."

The pride on Brian's face made her nod instead of finishing her sentence. He had misunderstood her offer, but his response would be the same. He didn't want to connect into the local social services, and unless Nick seemed endangered, she had no reason to push him. Sure, their life was hard, but it was their life.

"I'll just show myself out," she said instead.

"Hold on. I'll walk you to your house. It's dark out there."

Celia shook her head and laughed. "I can manage in Foster's Way. You take care of Nick. He'd be frightened to wake up in here with no one at home."

Brian came across the room toward her, clearly planning a protest, but Celia thrust out her hand for a shake. "Thank you for the lesson," she said, keeping her tone formal. "I enjoyed it."

His long, articulate fingers wrapped around hers and she shivered as her skin absorbed his warmth. His eyes glinted, and for a heartbeat, she thought he'd pull her in closer.

Then the moment passed.

He released her hand and smiled a gentle smile. "Until next time then."

Celia nodded and turned to make her escape, acutely aware how he'd followed her out into the hallway and to the front door.

"Bye for now," she called over her shoulder as she pushed past the entrance. She didn't hear the door close behind her and somehow knew he stood at the opening watching until she turned the corner.

Her lips curved into a smile and anticipation washed over her. Only one week until her next lesson. One week and she'd have an excuse to see him again.

Chapter 16

Brian shook his head, half laughing when he discovered his hand poised in the air guitar position again. Lyrics had been teasing at him all morning.

"I have no concentration today," he told the empty dining room, his words coming out muffled behind the mask he wore.

The plaster under the wallpaper had been saturated as well. Making this room livable would take more work than anything else in the old house, but he wanted it done. He wanted to invite Celia into his house without worrying about what might be hiding behind one of the doors.

His lips pulled down as he remembered her expression the first time. Even though he'd tried to dismiss her as a busybody back then, he could still feel the shame and could only imagine what she'd thought...what she might still think.

Brian dug his scraper against the wall, gouging out a hunk of plaster. That woman snuck into his thoughts all too often for his peace of mind, and yet somehow, he felt more alive and aware when thinking of her.

He ran a hand through his hair, fingers tangling on the mask strap.

Brian didn't need this kind of complication right now. Between the house, raising Nick, and giving up performing, he had enough to deal with.

His eyes slipped closed and a smile curved his lips at the memory of last night. His fingers still itched for the feel of steel beneath them, but lacked the edge of desperation he'd felt growing within him. Brian didn't have to give up music, shouldn't give up music, just because he couldn't perform. He'd been foolish to think so.

No one knew he was here. He'd covered his tracks well, dropped out with no warning despite his agent's protests, and he'd left no trail for the reporters to follow. Another reason he chose to move Nick.

What kind of life would his son have, always followed by journalists trying to get into Brian's head. It would never have ended.

But he didn't have to give up the music.

Hearing the thought for a second time galvanized Brian. He lowered the scraper, dusted his hands and pants as best he could, then stripped off the mask. "Nick," he called, having sent his son off for a break after a hard morning. "How'd you like a playing session?"

The sound of thumping footsteps reached his ears before Brian had made it halfway across the room.

"Play what?" Nick asked, poking his head around the door. In the next second, his nose wrinkled, and he stepped back.

Brian laughed. "I guess I've gotten used to the smell. I hardly notice it anymore."

Nick shook his head. "Well, it's still there. And it stinks. I don't think Celia likes it either."

Brian stopped just before the door and stared at his son. He wanted to ask why Celia's impression mattered, why Nick cared, but he kept the words to himself. Apparently she'd worked her magic on his son as much as she'd wriggled her way into his thoughts.

"So what are we going to play? Catch? Frisbee?"

"Oh." To Brian, play meant only one thing. And Lullaby Lady called to him with a siren's song. "Maybe we can do those later, or another day."

The disappointment on Nick's face made him want to reconsider. The music could wait.

"I suppose you want me to go back to scraping then," Nick said, his voice subdued but with none of the angry resentment they'd shared before.

Lullaby Lady's return had given Brian so much. With aching slowness, he had started to forge connections with his son that held none of the mix of guilt and anger they'd struggled with since he picked Nick up after the funeral.

Brian had been so distracted by Nick's tone it took a moment for the words to sink in.

"Oh, no." He shook his head. "I didn't mean to get to work. I was thinking another session with the guitar. You could have something to show Celia for her next lesson." And I could spend some time making music, he added to himself.

A grin split Nick's face. "That would be great! She got a better lesson than me anyway because I had to go and fall asleep." His expression twisted, but he couldn't hold the scowl for long. He grabbed Brian's hand and pulled him toward the parlor.

"Wait. Wait, Nick. I have to get washed up and now so do you. You wouldn't want Lullaby Lady harmed by all this plaster, would you?"

Nick glanced down at the white powder that seemed to creep up his wrist from where he'd caught hold of Brian's hand and shook his head vigorously.

"Oh no, I wouldn't want that," he said in a serious tone. "Especially not plaster from in here."

If not for the pungent dust on his hands, Brian would have tousled Nick's hair. He felt the connection swelling and growing between them, something more wondrous than he'd ever felt.

"You use the downstairs bathroom, then. I'll run a quick shower and be down to join you in a moment." He took two steps toward the stairs, then paused and glanced back. "You can even take her out and start practicing if you're careful."

Nick rewarded his words with another grin. Brian continued up the stairs, a smile of his own growing broader. He should have known music would be a connection.

After a quick shower, Brian was gratified to hear music coming from the parlor, clumsy chords, but with clear effort behind them. He jumped the last few steps, landing harder than he'd planned.

The music stopped.

"Are you okay?" Nick's voice came from the open door.

Brian grimaced, then laughed. "Yeah, I'm fine. Just not as young as I once was."

Nick gave him a look that seemed to wonder if he had ever been young as Brian came around the door and crossed to where the chairs were still set up.

Three chairs.

His gaze drifted to the third one, and he felt Celia's absence even though she'd only been there once. This gift, the rediscovery of his music, had been inspired by her; she was an integral part of it. Somehow, it felt wrong that she wasn't there.

He turned away and sank down into his chair to watch Nick struggle through the first chords he'd taught them.

"Slide your fingers closer to the fret and press tight. It'll clear up some of the buzz."

Nick frowned in concentration and shifted his fingers with a squeal of metal.

His next chord sounded cleaner, but before Brian could congratulate him, Nick dropped his left hand and shook it. "You play for a while. My fingers hurt."

He lifted Lullaby Lady into the air and Brian took her before she could fall, stifling the command to keep practicing.

"You need to build up calluses. Once you have them, as long as you keep playing, they'll protect your fingers from the strings and you can play longer."

Nick blew on his fingers, the tips red and shiny, a clear sign he'd been practicing for a while before Brian had returned. "I can practice a little every day. Then maybe it won't hurt so much."

Brian laughed. "No pain, no gain? Yeah, if you practice every day, even just a little, you'll get the protective shields over your fingertips. It's a sound plan."

Nick nodded and turned up his grin. "But now it's your turn. You don't practice nearly enough. You play."

Biting back the statement that he didn't need to practice if he wasn't performing, Brian gave a rueful smile. He couldn't blame Nick for his decision, and he shouldn't be so touchy about it either. Especially not now.

His fingers wrapped around Lullaby Lady's neck, and his other arm curled over her body. For Nick, he could do something he hadn't dared to in front of Celia. He could play some of his own songs.

Without thinking, he played a song he'd written a few months after Nick had been born. The notes of *A Son of My Own* drifted from the strings, and he added his voice to the mix, telling of how the miracle of birth had stunned and humbled him.

"It's about me, isn't it?" Nick asked as the last note died out, his eyes wide.

Brian stared at his son, still caught up in the emotions of the long-ago time. Then he shook his head to clear it and smiled. "Yeah, it is. I wrote the song when you were just a baby, and I thought I had your whole life ahead of me."

Nick nodded, seeming to hear the tinge of bitterness in Brian's tone despite his efforts to hide it.

"But now you do," his son said, the words too wise for such a small frame.

"You're right." This time Brian didn't squelch the desire to brush his fingers over Nick's head. "Now I do."

"Play another of your songs," Nick demanded, leaving no room for a refusal.

Brian wondered for a moment how Nick had known the song was about him, how he'd recognized it as one of Brian's songs. But then, his son had been in school, he'd had friends who might have listened. Kaitlin couldn't have controlled Nick's whole life, not now that he was older.

The strings reverberated with a swell of sound as Brian strummed across them, then he sank into a complicated picking sequence. He wished he could share his own songs with Celia as well. He could imagine her soft smile and wide eyes staring at him as he serenaded her the way he'd sung to Kaitlin long before their lives had broken apart.

Brian's fingers stilled, the words stopped coming from his lips, and he stared out the window, not seeing anything.

Part of him couldn't believe Celia hadn't recognized him, or at least his singing voice. He'd prided himself on his distinctive tones; critics had raved about his voice often enough. But at the same time, it had been too long since someone accepted him for himself and not the famous name, the stage presence.

Even Kaitlin had fallen first for the star. They'd met after a coffee house performance when they were still in high school. Not much of a star, but enough to capture her attention. She'd come to resent that part of him later when she had to live with it, especially after he'd gained nationwide attention.

Celia seemed to like him, which was nice, more than nice. And he didn't want to spoil it by playing something she could recognize.

Once she knew, she'd be like all the others.

They couldn't help it. It came with the territory. And it would mess up everything he was trying to do here.

"Aren't you going to finish the song?" Nick asked, the impatience in his tone a clear sign Brian had drifted for a while.

"Of course. Just one more though. I'm getting tired."

He almost sighed when the words slipped from his throat. He wasn't tired. He could go on playing for hours and only soothe a fraction of his need for music. He wasn't tired of playing; he was tired of having his life judged by a choice made when he was too young to understand the implications. No, he didn't want to give up music, or even to give up the music scene forever, but sometimes he just wanted to be a guy interested in getting to know a girl.

Chapter 17

M elanie, do you know anything about country music?" Celia asked as they shelved the latest magazines on Monday morning. She caught the look of surprise on her coworker's face before the other girl smothered it.

"What? Is it that awful?" She thought about the last song Brian had played and a flash of annoyance ripped through her at Melanie's attitude.

With a shake of her head, Melanie laughed. "Oh, not at all. I like a ton of country music. It's just…well, you don't seem the type. I'd expect you to prefer classical if anything. You've never seem to notice the music I play for the store."

Laughing at how quick she'd been to be offended, Celia shook her head. "I don't know how much classical I've heard. I never paid much attention to music. It's just there, in the background. Like a movie soundtrack."

Not that she'd seen many movies either. She stood still for a moment, contemplating how empty of what most considered standard her existence had been.

"So why the sudden interest?" Melanie ducked under the main counter, not bothering with the section that lifted any more than she ever did. She turned the key on the register, letting it wake up again with a series of sharp pings. "You sweet on some guy who likes music?"

"Of course not. I'm just curious." Celia added the last, aware her ready protest would just provoke more teasing and hoping to distract.

"A guitar, a sudden curiosity about country…you're being all too mysterious."

Celia joined Melanie at the counter, leaning over from the customer side. "Don't put too much meaning into it. I'm taking lessons, remember? I told you about them. It's just my teacher prefers country."

Melanie put a hand over Celia's and pulled her lips into a mock frown. "You should never fall for the teacher, dear. It's inappropriate."

A full laugh burst from Celia at Melanie's impression of one of their frequent customers. "Mrs. Shiner would never be so personal," she managed through her giggles.

Melanie shook her head. "Just give her a couple more months. It starts all cozy with suggestions on how to order the mysteries, but it never lasts. She went from 'helping' with the cookbooks to asking about my boyfriend. Now, she's waiting for an invitation to the wedding." The girl frowned. "A little hard since the boy she thinks I'm seeing doesn't know I exist."

"You didn't."

"I did. I just wanted to get her off my back. Next thing I know, it's wedding bells." Melanie sighed. "At least she doesn't gossip. For a while there, I feared his mom would come looking for me for details."

Celia straightened a display she'd bumped, not looking at Melanie. "I never really believed it about small towns, but everyone really does know everyone else's business."

"Yeah. It can be annoying, but you'll never feel lost here. Someone will be happy to point the way."

"Did you ever go to a city, Melanie?" Something in the other girl's voice made Celia wonder.

Melanie grimaced. "I went. All kids want to run from the small towns, to see the big city and leave this behind. I didn't like what I saw there. I spent half a semester at State. The teachers didn't even bother to learn our names, though how they could with four hundred students in each class I don't know. I decided it was better to be welcome in a small community than lost in a huge one."

Celia didn't have to think to bring the feeling back around her. The impersonal nature of a city could get to a person even when it had been all she'd ever known.

"Oh, you are good," Melanie said, a grin suddenly appearing on her face. "But not good enough. I see right through your trickery. I want to know all about this guitar man you've found."

Celia shrugged, more to push aside memories of her past than in response to Melanie. "I don't really know much about him. He plays guitar, country by preference, and he has a kid."

"A kid, huh? What about the mother?"

"She's dead. Look, it really doesn't matter, does it? I just thought it would help my lessons if I knew some of the music he prefers. He's dredging up old folksongs for me, and many I don't even know."

Melanie crouched down and Celia heard the clack of plastic cases. "Okay, if it's country you want, it's country you'll get. Toby Keith good for you?"

"Sure. Anyone would do, I guess."

The music that had been playing stopped, and Celia heard a swishing sound before a man's voice blared out of the speakers singing about a woman driving a big old truck. She let the music wash over her, picking up some of the notes behind the vocals.

"So, what do you think?"

"I think my teacher sings better," Celia said, meaning it for a joke. At the same time, it did feel as though Brian's voice held something more. For her, at least.

Melanie laughed. "I'll leave the CD in. Maybe he'll grow on you...like this teacher of yours seems to have."

"Maybe he will."

"You'd look good in a plaid shirt and cowboy hat. Really sweet. What are they called? Bunnies or something?"

Celia knocked Melanie on the shoulder. "Yeah, well, I'm a bit tougher than your average fluffy bunny."

Melanie rubbed her arm, pretending to be in pain. "That's for sure. More like a jackrabbit."

"I know someone who will be hopping mad if we don't finish off the magazine rack."

Melanie turned to look at her and they both said, "Mrs. Shiner," before dissolving into laughter.

When they'd recovered from their giggles, Melanie pocketed the register key, and joined Celia at the magazine rack.

Celia thought the discussion over, but Melanie glanced at her and said, "Whatever he means to you, you've been happier than I've ever seen you since you found that guitar."

Celia only smiled in response, but the comment stuck with her through the whole day. At odd moments, she found herself thinking about Brian and humming *Gone Country*. She couldn't deny she enjoyed learning to play so far, and the company that came with it. Celia just didn't think it meant anything more. What did they have in common anyway?

WHEN BRIAN SAID THEY NEEDED to get down to work the next Friday, after the three of them had polished off another pizza, Celia hadn't known well enough to be scared. But now, hours later, her back ached and her fingers throbbed.

Gone was the musician, and in his place, came a taskmaster.

Celia twisted her mouth into a wry grin and took the moment he turned away as a chance to blow on her hot fingertips. She'd asked him to teach her, and teach her he was. Nick had skipped beyond her in the intervening week, and now she struggled to keep up.

"What are you doing?"

He'd caught her when she wasn't paying attention. Celia flushed, trying to come up with an explanation that wouldn't sound whiney.

Brian grabbed her hand and stared down at fingers worked so hard heat radiated from each tip. At least they proved she'd been trying.

"You little fool," he whispered, pulling Celia out of her sour thoughts. "Why didn't you say anything? You'll be lucky if you can play by your next lesson."

Celia flushed again, but this time for a different reason. He knelt before her, his face close and his eyes staring right into hers.

"I didn't want to disappoint you." The truth sounded silly now, but she hadn't known any better.

He blew cold air over her fingers.

She shivered with the contrast between her flaring nerves and the chill as he blew again.

"When I said you had to work, I didn't mean like this." Brian released her hand and pushed to his feet. "You have to have determination to keep at it so you will form calluses. But if you bruise or blister your fingers, even if you manage a callus, it will just peel off. Don't ever suffer like this in silence."

Celia hung her head, ashamed she'd thought he wanted her to keep going. She should have known better, should have said something.

"She didn't know. She's new at this."

Nick's higher voice brought her head back up, and she almost laughed to see him standing up to his father, the contrast in their forms denying Nick's parentage.

"We should have told her."

Brian shook his head and glanced down at Celia. "You're right. We should have told you. I forget what it's like to start out."

Celia smiled to show she'd taken no offence even as she contemplated a nice, cold icepack to soothe her fingers.

"How old were you when you learned how to play?" The question burst out, one she hadn't intended to voice, but Melanie's comments about how little she knew, dropped here and there over the whole week, gnawed at her.

He laughed, clearly not offended by her curiosity as some might have been. "I started with drums at about Nick's age. I like to make noise. My mother took me to the store to get a guitar within a month, wanting peace and quiet. The drum set went to a pawnshop a few days after Lullaby Lady stole my heart."

Celia stroked the curve of the guitar, trying to imagine a much younger Brian cradling the instrument in his arms.

"I guess it was love at first sight," she murmured.

His gaze caught hers for a long moment, then he looked away. "I guess it was. And a love that's lasted longer than most marriages."

She lifted the guitar off her lap and crossed to the case to put it back. The edge of bitterness in his tone only showed her she'd outstayed her welcome. She had no business prying into his past.

"I guess I'll be going then. I've done enough damage to my fingers for one night." She tried for a weak laugh.

Brian appeared at her side before she'd noticed him moving. He took the guitar from her and tucked it into the case the way a father might tuck in his child. But when he looked up at her, his expression was certainly not paternal.

"Do you have to go?" he asked, his deep voice sending shivers down her spine.

Celia glanced toward the window, noticing the sun had just started to sink. "It's getting late. If I leave now, I'll be home before the real dark."

"Nick has told me how much fun it is to play games with you in the park."

She looked at him, surprised at the comment. "What?"

"Well, I was thinking, since we had to stop early, we could play something…checkers, chess, backgammon?"

A sweep of the room revealed Nick had vanished, leaving her alone with his father. A man who, she'd noticed, had taken to a greater level of cleanliness for her visits. She shifted her feet, suddenly uncomfortable. Was Melanie right? Had she fallen for her teacher?

"You don't have to stay long. I thought it would be a nice end to the day. If you don't want to…"

Something in his voice made her pause, and she glanced back to see a pleading look on his face. Though the expression was intended as a mockery, the emotion in his eyes seemed true.

"You really do want me to stay?"

"I do."

Tension thrummed in the air between them until Celia would have given anything to break it.

"I challenge you to a game of backgammon. Nick doesn't like it, and it's my favorite."

Even as she laughingly agreed, Celia missed the energy that had hung in the air for a minute. But did she want to take on someone as complicated as Brian? And how would any move on her part affect Nick?

Celia shook her head clear of the thought and followed Brian into the kitchen.

When she crossed the threshold, though, she discovered she'd fallen into a trap. Nick sat at the kitchen table, the checkerboard in front of him already set up with the pieces.

Brian had been helping his son. Any tension she'd felt between them had been one-sided.

"Did she agree?" Nick asked, excitement coloring his tone.

Brian swept past Celia, pausing long enough to hug her around the shoulders. "She did. But to backgammon. None of those checkers you use to plague me. And I'm going to get a cold cloth for her fingers first."

Nick's lips pursed into a pout. "Really?" he asked, his question directed at Celia.

She shrugged and grinned, knowing he wasn't complaining about the delay. "He challenged me to a game or two. Maybe after, there'll be time for checkers as well."

Her heart warmed at the sight of Nick's cheeky smile and the approval in Brian's expression when he handed her the cloth. She hadn't felt this good since as far back as she could remember. She could get used to this. It didn't matter if Brian seemed oblivious to the tension between them. Well, it didn't matter much.

Chapter 18

C elia puttered around her cottage on Saturday morning, picking up and cleaning. The pure domestic bliss made her laugh, but this had little to do with frantic attempts to stem the flow of city grime in her apartment before she ran out to check on her charges.

Life was different here. And she liked it.

She sank onto one of her kitchen chairs and looked out the window, drawn by the cheerful cries of the children who played some homegrown version of soccer out on the street. A hum started under her breath, and it took Celia a moment to recognize one of the few songs Brian had played for her the previous night. She tapped her fingers gingerly on the table, then moved them into chord positions, the practice coming almost automatically now. Her fingers hadn't blistered, but they still were sensitive and not up to much direct contact.

Restless, Celia stood up and crossed to the window to see the game. She pushed her memory to bring up more than just the faint bit of tune she hummed. Nothing came. She couldn't remember what he'd said the title was, who wrote it, or anything specific.

Turning away from the window, she sighed.

If she could only call Melanie, her coworker would probably have an answer in a heartbeat. Neither of them worked on the weekends, time reserved for high school kids. Their boss had done things that way for years, and as she'd told Celia when she hired her, why change a good thing?

If only Celia had gone out with Melanie any of those times the younger woman had offered. Then she'd have a way to contact her outside of work. Melanie could stop this earworm.

Or she could go to Brian's house.

The thought made her freeze. She remembered how he'd looked, how the house had been, when she showed up unannounced. He'd made great strides. She didn't want to be the one to undercut his growing confidence, especially not for something so simple. She'd see him on Friday after work. It had to be soon enough.

Celia put a kettle on and glowered at it.

For all she'd settled in here, she hadn't made any real friends in Foster's Way, no one she could go to when she felt the need to talk. She'd never had real friends, but she'd always blamed her circumstances. What better ones could she hope for than here?

The whistle startled her out of her thoughts, and Celia laughed aloud.

"A watched pot boils even faster than I could imagine," she told the empty room. "At least with distracting thoughts."

She poured water over the teabag she'd put in a mug earlier. The teapot she'd bought when she arrived still sat unused and neglected on the shelf. Why make a pot just for her? She'd never had a single visitor, unless the woman who came selling cookies with her daughter counted. They wouldn't come inside, though. Too many houses to visit.

Mug in one hand, Celia crossed to the table and sank down again.

"I could invite Melanie," she murmured, "or Nick and Brian. Though I doubt they'd be all that interested in tea."

She shook her head, knowing she wouldn't dare. Even though Brian had asked her to stay longer, Friday nights seemed timeless, separate from her normal life. If she broke the unspoken rules by asking them to visit, it felt like nothing would be the same ever again.

"That's straight out of fantasy," she told herself, grinning all the while at the image. "I've seen both Brian and Nick outside of the confines of their house."

The memories didn't help at all.

Brian hadn't looked the same outside. Within his house, prepared for the lesson, he was focused, dynamic, compelling...clean. Outside, she'd compared him to a Charlie Brown character, and not a particularly flattering one.

She noticed herself humming again, the same song as before. How could she find out what it was now? Celia didn't think she had the patience to wait for Monday, or even worse, all the way until Friday.

Celia pushed back from the table, her lips curving into a smile. She had a radio. It had come with the cottage. A clock radio. She only used the alarm setting, but the other must work; it had to.

The mechanism seemed simple enough when she flopped down on the bed and pulled the radio off the bedside table, but no music played when she pressed the button. After a bit of poking and prodding, she noticed a dial hidden on the side opposite the volume.

She turned it slowly, and an awful screech erupted from the little box. Celia dropped the radio in surprise. It bounced twice and toppled off the side of the bed, still crying out in a mix of static and hisses.

The noise battered her ears, never stopping until she rolled off the bed and walked around it to find the radio hanging from its power cord. She knew the volume dial well enough to return the box to a tolerable level, then set out to find a music station with single-minded concentration.

The first station she found blared out the sound of trumpets and violins, nothing like what she sought. The second was busy promoting a new dress shop downtown, and she turned past it as well.

The next clear station held voices, and she almost kept going, but a fragment of the words caught her attention:

...country music. He was a steady success, not too many chart toppers, but certainly expected a longer career. And yet he just vanished. His agent isn't talking and no one else seems to know what's going on either. What could have sent a musician of his talent away at the height of his career?

Celia put the radio back on the table and turned up the volume, wincing at the noise. They had to stop talking sometime, and she didn't want to stay in the bedroom. If they were giving country music news, the station clearly played country music.

Sure enough, by the time she'd gone into the kitchen and taken a sip of her tea, music poured out from the bedroom. Celia grinned. She could get used to this kind of music.

The morning chores went by faster as she hummed along with the radio even though they never played the song she'd been listening for. Celia couldn't understand why she'd lived in silence since coming here, though the constant music at the store might have had something to do with it. The rap and hard rock her charges loved never really caught her imagination. Leaving it behind had been a relief, but she could have turned on a radio; she could have figured out what she liked.

Buying that guitar had been one of the best things she'd ever done.

On her own, it would have sat in the corner, her feeble efforts never bringing her joy. But with Brian's help, she felt as if her eyes had opened to a whole new world. She couldn't wait for her next lesson. How Brian would laugh to hear her thrilling over something as simple as turning on a radio to a station of her choice.

He might be struggling, but his life was golden compared to her self-imposed isolation.

"Come on, Nick. You can throw it harder than that," Brian teased, backing up the length of the yard for the third time.

His son grinned at him before taking off at a run with the ball clutched to his chest.

"Hey, no fair." His speed hampered by laughter, Brian charged after Nick.

The boy sprinted around the side of the house, twisted between the plastic garbage cans, and burst onto the sidewalk in time to startle their neighbor out walking her twin Pekinese. The dogs strained at their leashes and pierced eardrums with their sharp yips.

Brian cleared the cans just in time to see the almost collision. "Look, I'm sorry he bothered you. Nick, you need to pay better attention to where you're going."

"Oh, leave the boy alone," the white-haired lady told him. "I've raised seven of them in my day, and he's no worse than any of mine."

She turned as Nick asked a question Brian was too far away to hear.

"Yes, you can pet them. They're kid friendly, though you're smart to ask."

The woman smiled at Brian. "I'm just happy to see you doing something with this old place. Horrid how the family let it go to rot after Elspeth died. She would have wept to see the condition of her home."

Brian gave her a smile, stunned at how nice she was. He'd assumed something far different than keeping an eye on an old friend's place from the few times he'd seen her peering out from her own home. "You knew her, then? It's a wonderful old house."

"I'll tell her you said so."

The woman laughed aloud at what must have crossed his expression. "In my prayers, dear. That's how we old folk keep up with our friends who've passed."

She winked at him, and he didn't know whether to take her seriously or consider it a joke.

"Well, I won't keep you two. I just wanted you to know I appreciated your efforts here."

She tugged gently on the leashes, and both dogs barked once then scampered out ahead of her as if they knew what the signal meant.

"Wait," Brian called. "I'm Brian. This is Nick," he said, waving at his son.

The woman laughed again and shook her head. "I must be getting on in years. I'm Mrs. Michaels, Sarah. I run the bakery on Main Street. Stop in some time. I make the best creampuffs you've ever tasted."

"Nice to meet you, Mrs. Sarah Michaels. We'll do that some time."

"Make sure you do," she said before continuing down the street.

Nick put his hand into Brian's, and Brian closed his fingers around it.

"She sure seems nice, doesn't she?"

"Yeah, she does. A lot of nice people in Foster's Way."

Nick tugged toward the house. "But I think Celia's nicer," he said as they reached the steps leading to their front door.

"Hmm," Brian managed, holding back his instinctive agreement. "It's not a contest."

Celia spent too much time in his thoughts as it was. He didn't need to be comparing every female he came across to her.

"Hey, you getting hungry? We could have a picnic out in the backyard."

"Can we?" Nick pushed the unlocked door open. "That would be great. I'll get the food."

Brian stared after his son.

Why had he taken so long just to spend time with Nick? Had making the house look a little nicer really made a difference?

Hadn't Nick needed him more than the parlor did, no matter what Mrs. Michaels might have said?

He let the door close behind him, but he didn't see the empty corridor. He saw the look on Celia's face when she'd opened the still unfinished dining room instead.

Well, maybe some work on the house had been necessary. Without the parlor, he'd have had no place for the lessons. And without them, Brian wondered if he'd be as comfortable around Nick as he'd become.

As much as Brian hated to admit it, the reason Celia kept coming into his thoughts was because she'd influenced him more than he wanted to consider. She'd transformed what could have been a disaster into a connection with his son when she returned the guitar. The lessons had been one of the first ways he'd spent time with Nick that wasn't working on the house. No wonder his son had been resistant and grumpy.

"Wouldn't it be nice if Celia was here," Nick said as Brian stepped into the kitchen. "She could share in the picnic."

Brian shook his head, unsurprised his son's thoughts had followed a similar path. He put his hands on Nick's shoulders and turned the boy away from the sandwiches he'd been making.

"She has her own life to live, Nick. We can't expect her to devote all her free time to us. It wouldn't be fair. And I don't want you hurt. I know it has to be rough without your mother here, but we do alright, don't we?"

For a moment, it looked like liquid built up in Nick's eyes, but his son blinked back the tears.

"Celia isn't my mother. I know that," he said. "I just like her, okay?"

Brian sighed. "Yeah, it's okay. I like her too. I just don't want you counting on her. She doesn't owe us a thing."

Nick nodded. "But I think she likes us, too," he said after a moment.

Brian laughed, the sound bursting out of him. "I certainly hope so," he told his son, rubbing a hand across Nick's head.

"Stop it! You'll mess it all up," Nick cried, trying not to laugh himself.

"Oh, it isn't close to being a mess, yet." Catching his son under one arm, Brian held him up while he finished the job Nick's wild run had started.

"Now that's what I'd call messy," he said after setting Nick back on the floor.

Nick used both hands to press his hair down, but the grin on his face showed he'd enjoyed the moment.

"Now I'm starving. How about I help you with the sandwiches?"

"Well, I don't know," Nick said, still grinning. "You know how to use a knife?"

"Good enough to spread peanut butter at least," Brian answered. His heart swelled at the thought of a lifetime of these little moments. He didn't want to waste even a second. He'd missed so many already.

Chapter 19

Her fingers sank into long black hair. She tugged him down to her, savoring the desire in his deep brown eyes. Their lips met, and his hand stroked the length of her, bringing her body to life.

Celia shifted away from the patch of sunlight bathing her face. She rolled over, reaching for Brian.

Her fingers closed on an empty pillow.

Startled, Celia blinked awake. Heat raced up her cheeks and across her breasts.

…singing Her Sweet Kisses. Just like the woman in his song, this singer has vanished from the scene. We will miss his sweet voice.

Another country song started, and Celia laughed. She must have turned the alarm to music in all her fumbling on Saturday. The church bells always woke her on Sunday, so she hadn't used the alarm. There'd been no way to discover the change until this morning.

The lyrics pouring out of the radio caught her attention, and she stopped to listen until the song ended.

You've been listening to Rodney Adkins and I've Been Watching You, a song about a father's love for his son.

Songs like this one must have given Brian hope. Despite the jokes about country music, she'd found only some of the songs she'd heard dealt with loss. There were as many about faith, family, and love.

The thought of love made her cheeks heat again. She must have incorporated the songs into her dreams, and who else would star in it? Mr. Peterson? She really didn't know any men around her age except Brian and the few who stopped by the bookstore.

Celia rubbed a hand across her face, trying to wipe away the lingering touch of her dream. She'd have the better part of a week to forget it before she saw Brian again, but still, she worried it would be awkward.

Her glance coasted over the clock then jerked back.

"Not as awkward as showing up late for work on a Monday," she yelped, slapping the music off and climbing out of bed. She'd never slept through the loud beeping, but apparently listening to music appealed more than breakfast.

In the rush to wash up, get dressed, and gulp down some yogurt, Celia pushed the dream from her thoughts, but the effort didn't last.

Melanie gave her more than one odd look when she felt a blush heating her face over the next few days, but Celia offered no explanation. She would have to stop this, or she'd never survive her next lesson.

Chapter 20

B rian stepped back, his head a little dizzy despite the mask and all the open windows. He'd been working hard ever since Saturday, but with Friday coming up, time had run short. He glanced around the room and grinned.

"I can't believe it. It's done."

He laughed aloud and stared at the dining room, comparing the disgusting, piss-soaked trash heap where a vagrant or stray dogs had nested to the elegant, turn-of-the-century room he had uncovered.

A heartbeat later, he tore off his mask, put down the stiff-bristled brush he'd been using to apply maple stain, and rushed out of the room.

"Nick, where are you? You've got to see this."

He ran up the stairs, expecting to find his son playing on the game machine again, but Nick wasn't there. He wasn't in the parlor practicing the guitar, either.

Brian sucked in a breath, forcing down instinctual panic. He'd asked Nick to tell him before leaving the house, but Nick was just a kid. He could have forgotten. It was the middle of the afternoon. What could happen, anyway?

A triumphant shout came from the direction of the kitchen, and Brian shook his head.

He didn't know how other parents managed this constant barrage of fears, but he didn't regret taking Nick with him. He hadn't known how lonely he'd been surrounded by all those people in country music. Not one of them, not even his agent, really gave a damn about him.

Nick actually cared.

Dropping into an easy stride, he crossed from the parlor, through the hallway, and into the kitchen, expecting to find Nick had concocted some new delicacy he'd have to stomach. The combinations his son could still call food were amazing—when they didn't churn in his gut.

But the kitchen stood as empty as the other rooms had been. Only the open back door gave Brian a clue. Feeling a little like a mouse following a trail of crackers, he approached the open door cautiously.

Had Nick planned a trick or something?

The sight that greeted his eyes froze Brian for only a heart-beat before a smile stretched his mouth until his cheeks ached.

"You practicing up for our next bout?" he called.

The ball slipped from Nick's startled fingers, and his son turned to face Brian. "You said I couldn't throw any better than you can. You'll never say so again. Just watch."

Nick scooped up the ball and ran to the far side of the yard before he stopped.

Brian moved down the steps, but Nick shook his head.

"No, stay right there."

With a thought to how Mrs. Michaels would react to a ball landing in her begonias, Brian settled on the top step.

Nick waved his hand back once, twice, then a third time before he let go.

Brian watched the arc of the ball as it soared across the lawn, much farther and firmer than the previous day. Then, he let out a startled laugh.

"Good job," Brian called, pushing to his feet to investigate the net Nick had put together. "Have you been practicing?"

"A bit." Nick ran up to him. "I'm getting good, aren't I?"

Brian reached down and swung his son into his arms for a hug. "You're doing great. Pretty soon we'll have to go down to the park to play catch. This yard won't be wide enough."

"Can we go now? Celia might be there."

Brian ignored the tightening of his chest and the sudden longing to agree. Instead, he lowered Nick to the ground and ruffled the boy's hair.

"Silly, she's probably working. We'll see her on Friday."

"Yeah, I suppose so." Nick didn't sound quite as enthusiastic as a moment before.

"You want to see my surprise," Brian said, more to distract both Nick and himself than because of any urgency. "I finished the dining room."

"Really?" Nick's energy returned with a surge, and he raced for the house.

Brian followed after, stunned at his son's reaction. Had the room bothered the boy as much as it had him? They might have started to talk, but it was obvious they hadn't communicated some of the big stuff.

By the time he caught up, Nick had already barged into the room. The stench of maple stain lingered in the air, but it didn't seem to bother Nick as he turned slowly to take in the whole effect.

"Wow. You did a great job."

Brian grinned, unaware until that moment how much Nick's approval meant to him. The boy's eyes were wide and a matching grin split his face.

"So you like it?" Brian asked.

"It's wonderful. It doesn't stink anymore." Nick took a deep breath, coughed, and shrugged. "Well, you know, like it did. And I like all the wood. Just wait until Celia sees this."

Brian wanted to protest, but he'd had the same feeling. He wanted to wipe out any bad memories she might have had of this place and of them. This room had been a big part of it. He wasn't done with the remodeling, but at least the whole house was habitable at last.

"We can show her before the lesson, right? Or even have it in here."

"I don't know if the stain will have all dried by then. We shouldn't stay in here too long with the smell."

Nick shook his head. "It's a good smell." Then he wrinkled his nose. "But it'll be gone by Friday, don't you think? If we leave the windows open? That's two whole days."

Brian laughed. "I hope so, but the paint in the other rooms took longer than I'd thought to dry. Better not to plan on it."

"Hmm. Well, we can still show her."

"Yeah, we will show it to her." He looked around the room, anticipating Celia's surprise and looking forward to her presence. He didn't understand how he could miss her—it had been less than a week—but he did.

Brian shook his head in a feeble attempt to clear his thoughts. "Tell you what. Let me go get washed up, then we'll take a run down to the park. You can show off your throwing arm, and maybe I can even catch a few."

Nick nodded. "Sure. Sounds great. I'll put together some food. We haven't eaten since lunch and that was hours ago."

Brian tried to laugh about Nick's preoccupation with eating as his son ducked under his arm and headed for the kitchen, but couldn't. Something had been missing from Nick's sentence, and only now did Brian realize how much he wanted to hear it.

Sounds great, Dad. That's what he used to tell his father. But Nick had never called him Dad. The few times he'd used a name, it was always Brian.

CELIA STARED AT HER HANDS, unable to remember a single chord, unable to curl her fingers into the right positions to practice. She slapped the kitchen table, knowing her inability had nothing to do with poor memory.

She'd dreamed of Brian again, shared deep kisses, felt him stroke her skin, and she'd spent all day at the bookstore trying not to remember, a difficult task with Melanie giving her inquisitive looks and offering to lend a friendly ear to her problems.

Celia's fingers twitched, not into the form of a simple A chord, but with a longing to touch him, to feel his skin beneath her sensitive fingertips. Only one more workday before her lesson. It seemed like an eternity.

She shoved back from the table and rose, filled with antsy energy that wouldn't let her settle, wouldn't let her concentrate. How would she be able to face Brian at the lesson? How could she feel his arms wrap around her and not lean into the touch?

"The first step is to turn off the blasted music," she told the kitchen, then marched into the bedroom.

At the last moment, Celia hesitated. She liked the sound of music bringing her slowly to awareness of the world even if it meant she had to set the alarm earlier. This had been lacking in her life here, and she didn't want to give it up.

Celia sank onto the bed and pulled a pillow against her chest. She'd never felt this way before, not about a man, not even in general. All these emotions were new to her.

She couldn't have grown up where she'd been, worked with the kids she had, without knowing the facts of life. But it had never touched her. She'd never wanted to join in.

"Delayed puberty, that's all this is. The music, the dreams. They don't mean anything." She threw the pillow away from her and reached for the switch again.

"But does that make it wrong?" Her finger paused a second time. "Don't I deserve my fantasies? Maybe it would have been a TV star, or a musician, if I ever saw them. Just because the man in my dreams looks like Brian doesn't mean it really is him."

She groaned, knowing full well her rationalizations were just that.

This time, her finger did reach the slide and she set it to the obnoxious noise that would keep her dreams free of confusion.

"Besides, as Melanie pointed out, having a crush on a teacher is a time-honored tradition. Doesn't have to mean anything more just because I'm older than a school girl."

The last bit actually reassured her. It wasn't as if Brian showed any real signs of interest in her anyway. When she thought he had, he'd been helping Nick, not wanting her. They were pupil and teacher, maybe even friends, but surely nothing more.

She pushed away the part of her that wished they were more than friends and surged to her feet. The excess energy demanded an outlet. She would jog it away and not have to worry about this anymore. It was a better idea than sitting around moping, at least.

Celia snagged her sack of game pieces in an afterthought. She might end up by the park, and Nick might be there looking for a game.

BRIAN BENT OVER, HIS HANDS on his knees, panting and laughing all at once.

"You almost had me that time," Nick said, dancing around in front of Brian. The grass barely had a chance to compress before Nick was off crushing a new spot with his sneakers.

Exaggerating for effect, or so he told himself, Brian staggered over to the game tables and sank down on a bench.

"How about we take a break," he called. "Relax a bit."

Nick gave a quick glance to the swings, then turned back to Brian and wandered over.

"You want to go to the playground? I can just sit here and get my breath in order."

The look on his son's face made Brian laugh and wave Nick off. "Go on. I'll be fine. Happy even."

He watched Nick alternate between racing and hopping over to the swings, stunned at the transformation from the quiet, withdrawn boy he'd picked up after the funeral. They'd started hanging out together, something he'd barely dreamed possible.

Brian laughed at the thought, his muscles aching from the ball toss followed by a race that had really been him chasing Nick around. If they kept going like this, he'd collapse. He would have thought all the work on the house had kept him in shape, but he could tell it was a lie.

Nick let out a shriek and Brian turned to watch him swing, higher, ever higher. Sure, he missed the adrenalin of the circuit, being the focus of attention, being on stage, but this offered something stronger.

He owed it all to Celia, the woman who had wrinkled her nose at the first sight of him. Brian's lips curved in a smile at the memory. Part of him had hoped to find her down here. He knew she'd caught Nick at the playground before, and he wanted to see her.

The smile turned into a laugh. Brian pivoted on the bench and ran his fingers over the fading paint of the checkerboard. He was no lovesick teenager to moan over her absence. It was already Thursday evening, and they had a standing date on Friday.

No, not a date, a lesson. A business arrangement. And he was too busy trying to settle into this new life for it to become anything more.

"Hi!"

Brian heard Nick's shout and turned, wondering if some other kid had come into the empty park. His heart clenched when he caught sight of who waved back.

Celia.

Even as she crossed to Nick's side, laughed when he launched himself from the still-moving swing, and then joined Nick as they walked this direction, Brian tried to puzzle out what it was about her. She seemed oblivious to him, but he savored every moment in her company.

Brian let out his breath on a sigh.

Maybe that was it. Maybe the answer to his attraction was as simple as finally meeting a woman who had no interest in him. Figured he'd come up with the perfect formula. He could pine in the distance and never worry about having to act on his feelings, worry about failing her as he had Kaitlin.

"Hi, Brian."

Her voice seemed cheerful, inviting, but he knew she didn't mean it the way he wanted—or didn't want.

"Would you like to play some checkers?" Nick broke in, dispersing the uncomfortable moment. "We don't have pieces, but rocks work."

Celia pulled a bag out of her pocket and shook it. "I have mine. Checkers sounds great." She paused and looked at Brian, her expression uncertain. "If it's okay with you? I mean, I'm not interrupting, am I?"

Brian shook his head, suddenly aware he'd been staring. He liked the way her hair brushed her neck, articulating her every move.

"No, no, that's fine. I'm still recovering from our run. You two play the first game, and I'll play the winner."

Celia slipped onto the bench opposite him, and Nick nudged Brian over so they could play. Brian tried not to read anything into the decision to use this board instead of leaving him on his own, but he had to force his gaze away from Celia's bent head as she sorted the checkers out from among her chess pieces.

He closed his eyes and focused on the earlier thought of how his attraction was because she was unattainable. He didn't want her to glance up with a spark of interest in those blue eyes. He didn't want his life any more complicated than it already was.

Despite his internal pep talk, though, it wasn't until Nick beat Celia soundly in a brilliant series of moves that Brian started focusing on the game. He laughed with the two of them, commiserated with Nick's latest victim, and rose, planning to take his place.

Celia rose too, as did Nick.

"I'll switch," his son said, again breaking a tension he couldn't be aware of.

For just a heartbeat, Brian wanted to protest he could share the bench with Celia. He wanted an excuse to press up against her, feel her softness at his side. Then, he shrugged. "Probably the best solution."

She glanced at him, but looked away before he could read her expression. Brian told himself to concentrate on the game so he didn't lose too badly, but envy for his twelve-year-old son kept distracting him.

Chapter 21

Celia tried to ignore the shiver of nerves as she walked up the street where Nick and Brian lived. Playing checkers with them in the park last night had not helped her distraction at all. Again, she'd woken with Brian's name on her lips, with his imagined touch lingering on her skin.

A flush heated her cheeks, and she stopped to catch her breath, struggling for control. Melanie had some sixth sense about her when thoughts of Brian rose. She'd spent the day laughing at Celia, not in a mean way, but enough to make the embarrassment sting all the more.

Celia turned away, fists clenched at her sides. She couldn't go there like this. She wasn't some kid gone starry-eyed over her teacher, and Brian wouldn't know how to turn her away gently. Celia didn't know which would be more embarrassing: acknowledgment or oblivion.

"Hey, Celia! You're late."

She glanced toward Nick's voice, feeling as if the choice had been taken from her hands. She forced a smile on her face, determined to keep the boy from seeing her inner turmoil.

"I guess I'm a slow walker," she managed, unable to come up with a reasonable excuse. Then she glanced down at her hand and groaned. She'd forgotten to pick up the pizza.

Nick's hand curled around her arm before she could turn and run. "Come on. Brian's waiting for you."

Distracted, she wondered if Brian had told Nick to use his first name, or if Brian longed to hear those simple three letters, only to be denied.

She shook her head. It was none of her business what Brian longed for.

"I forgot to pick up the pizza. I have to go back."

Nick had already run ahead, vanishing into the bowels of what had turned out to be a nice, welcoming place despite the disgusting room. Celia sighed and picked up her pace, knowing she'd be retracing these steps soon enough.

She closed the door behind her and started down the corridor only to freeze. Their voices came not from the kitchen, but from the nearer door, the door that had always been closed except for during her unfortunate decision to assess their living space. She'd had no business then, and no inclination now.

Nick stuck his head out. "Well? Aren't you coming?"

Unsure what drove her to this, Celia sucked in a deep breath and strode to the doorway, knowing she couldn't hold the air long enough no matter what she tried.

The room held a grinning Brian, a decent wood table, and real chairs.

Before she could turn purple, Celia released her breath only to find no noxious smell to assault her. Instead, the freshly applied stain offered a sharp, but pleasant, scent. She crossed the doorstep and looked around the room, amazed at how cared for it appeared. Brian and Nick had put a lot of work into this space, especially considering what it had been only a few weeks ago.

"So, do you like it?"

From the hint of impatience in Brian's tone, she guessed he'd been waiting on her reaction. Celia turned away to hide her smile and took an extra moment to really see the room.

Nick danced in front of her, and she winked, playing with Brian though she couldn't for the life of her tell why.

"She likes it," Nick said, spoiling her fun.

She guessed it was too much to ask that a twelve-year-old would understand what she didn't herself.

"It's beautiful," she said, turning to face Brian. "You've done a lot of work in here."

He nodded. "Of all the work this house needed, the dining room was the worst. But if you hadn't seen—smelled—it before, you'd have no idea."

Celia smiled in agreement, but her mind had taken off on other tracks.

From his comment, he wasn't responsible for the state of the house, something that matched her impression of the man much better than her first assumptions. What if a friend or relative had given him the place to clean up? It would have offered a focus as he got his act back together, and the giver would benefit by someday having a house to rent or sell.

Brian gave her an odd look, and once again, she remembered the pizza. "I forgot to pick it up. The pizza is made and everything." She didn't like feeling so flustered, but had only herself to blame. If she'd been focused on the lesson rather than facing Brian in light of her fantasies, she wouldn't have passed right by Giovanni's Pizza.

He looked surprised then nodded. "Don't worry. I can whip up some spaghetti quick enough. Use our phone to call and cancel the order."

"I can't do that." The exclamation burst from her lips before she could stop it, and she wondered again what world he had come from. She wouldn't go back on her word in ordering the pizza.

"Giovanni used time and ingredients on our meal. It's not fair to waste his efforts."

Only surprise showed on Brian's face now, another sign he'd never had to consider someone else. He must have been high on the corporate ladder, or someplace where they catered to his every need, before his fall. How difficult the transition must have been. Must still be. House restoration seemed as distant from a corporate life as from the life of the panhandler she'd first thought him to be.

"We could go eat there, couldn't we? It would be fun. Like a family outing."

Both of them turned to face Nick. Celia couldn't see Brian's expression, but she could feel the heat in her own.

"Sure," Brian said. "We could walk down there then come back for the lesson. I keep meaning to explore more of Foster's Way, but haven't had the chance. We've been to the other pizza place over by the Buy-Sell-Trade."

Celia let go of the breath she hadn't noticed holding. Had she wanted him to agree? To treat the three of them as some sort of family? Or had she wanted him to demand they pick it up and share the pizza in a more intimate setting?

Nick ran off after socks and shoes, Brian grabbed a denim jacket, and Celia just stood there, trying to find her way through the minefield of her emotions. What did she want from this man? And what did he want from her?

ONCE AGAIN, BRIAN HAD REASON to be jealous of his son, though he squashed the ungrateful thought.

Nick had walked between the two of them, holding their hands and swinging his own. The pizza parlor turned out to be a homely place filled with locals talking, laughing, and calling out to each other as if the separate tables were an inconvenience rather than an attempt at privacy. Everyone belonged.

The benches offered enough seating for four, and Nick had abandoned Brian in favor of the opposite side with Celia. It reminded him of the checkers game the previous night and how he'd wanted to be the one squished next to her. Brian glanced across their booth for the hundredth time, fighting the urge to tuck Celia's hair behind her ear, to gently cup her jaw and pull her close.

She looked up, and for a fleeting moment, he imagined her gaze held a touch of desire like must be mirrored in his own. Celia turned to say something to Nick, and Brian dismissed the thought as wishful thinking, at least until it happened again. Then he started to wonder if he was as alone in this attraction as he'd believed.

He had the perfect vantage point to watch the two special people in his life.

Brian choked on his drink as he heard the thought echo in his head. Nick was in his life. Celia only visited at best. He needed to remember that before he sank in too deep.

"Why are you staring at Celia?" Nick asked, once again oblivious to the tension between the two adults, or maybe all the tension came from Brian's side of the table.

"Do I have something on my face?" She turned toward his son in asking the question, rather than getting Brian's opinion.

Nick burst into laughter as her movement revealed her other cheek. "You are a mess," he told her in the blunt honesty of the young. "You have sauce all over your chin."

"Oh no." Though her words held a touch of embarrassment, Celia laughed as well, dragging a napkin under her lip then looking at it.

"You missed the spot," Brian said in a low voice. "It's more to your left side."

He kept one hand on his drink and the other on the pizza slice he'd been eating. If his hands were occupied, he wouldn't reach out to help her.

"And now?"

Again, she asked Nick rather than him, and this time, his son offered an approving smile.

"You got it."

Brian struggled with his imagination, half hoping she'd smear some more so he could come to the rescue no matter how ridiculous the wish. He muffled a groan with his pizza when the idea of a shared shower burst into his mind.

Nick started giggling again, this time at Brian. "You've got sauce on your nose," his son crowed.

Brian could only welcome the distraction as he dampened a napkin with his glass of water and wiped himself clean. "I think that's enough dinner for me. I'd prefer to eat it than wear it."

There'd been no bill. Celia had paid for the meal before they moved to claim a table since it had been take-out to start with.

Brian swore he'd repay her generosity in full measure, ignoring the little voice in the back of his head that pointed out how he'd earn many more dinners with her across from him in the process. Neither did he listen to the whisper suggesting he leave Nick behind when he did. If anything, thoughts of Nick gave him the strength to brush his attraction aside. He'd moved them here to get to know his son, not to abandon Nick the first time some woman made his blood pressure rise. Even if Celia was the woman in question.

Chapter 22

Celia spent dinner trying not to look at Brian, trying not to see him as the man haunting her dreams, and trying not to long for the real thing. He hadn't helped at all with the way she found him staring whenever she glanced up. Of course, he'd been looking at her messy face when she wanted to see desire in his gaze. Only Nick's presence saved the dinner, giving her an excuse not to embarrass herself over Brian.

On the way back to their house, Nick looped his arms through both of theirs, offering less separation than when they'd just been holding hands. Every time Brian laughed, Celia fought the need to turn and see the joy in his eyes. Humor meant for his son, not her.

She shook her head, telling herself to stop. She didn't need to complicate her life with someone not that much different from the charges she'd left behind. Brian had his own issues to sort out, and Celia couldn't afford the strain on her heart. She needed to keep things simple, and if she did look for a guy, he'd have nothing more pressing in his life than what to have for dinner.

"Coming in?"

Brian's laughing comment made her jerk her head up to find they'd reached the steps. She stood at the bottom, unmoving.

"Come on," Nick urged. "It's time for our lesson." The boy let loose a noisy burp then giggled.

Brian turned a stern, but loving, gaze on his son. "I told you the last piece was about three too many. When you crash, you're going down hard."

Nick glared back for a moment before grinning as he grabbed Celia's hand.

If she hadn't moved forward, she would have stumbled with his tug. Still, even if she could convince herself going home was the smart move, she'd made promises. She tried to keep hers. She'd seen what a lifetime of broken promises did to a person, knew it firsthand.

"I'm coming; I'm coming. I guess the pizza was a bit much for me, too." A yawn tugged at her mouth, but she fought it down. Her sleep had been too interesting of late to count as restful.

The thought sent her gaze skittering toward Brian, but he had already turned to go inside. She feasted on his lithe form, a rare opportunity without the risk of being caught. How could she have thought him a derelict before? He might have been dirty, but his every movement held power and control.

"He doesn't bite," Nick whispered loud enough for Brian to overhear.

Heat swept Celia's face, the blush growing hotter with Brian's bark of laughter. The urge to run only grew, but she gathered what remained of her dignity and stepped over the threshold. She prayed she'd be able to get through the night without making a complete fool of herself.

Celia stumbled through her lesson, shivering when Brian wrapped his arms around her, cradled her within them. Yet, whenever she faltered, he only touched her more, and Celia fought back the craving to make deliberate errors.

She closed her eyes to savor the hot, moist caress of his breath against her cheek, knowing she should concentrate. It proved more difficult than she'd feared to separate this Brian from the one sharing her dreams. He didn't make it any easier.

"Is everything alright?"

Brian's question jolted her out of a daze, and Celia blinked to see him kneeling in front of her, so close she could brush her mouth to his if only she leaned forward. Her tongue came out to wet her lips before she could stop it, and she felt the heat of another blush rising up her neck.

"It's fine," she managed. "Why do you ask?" Her voice sounded like a husky whisper, rather than her normal clear tone.

Brian reached up and tucked a strand of her hair behind her ear. "You just don't seem interested in the lesson tonight, that's all."

The blush grew hotter as she declared, "I am interested. Really, I am."

"Uh huh. And that's why your fingers can't find chords you knew on the first day."

She glanced down, unable to explain, unwilling to open herself to his ridicule, and worse, his rejection.

He put a finger under her chin and raised her face until it was level with his own. She waited for him to condemn her drive, to say anything, but he only leaned in, his body curved around the guitar in her arms.

She didn't have time to react before his lips met hers and a different kind of heat flooded her body. Her lips molded to his, and she moaned when he moved away only to have him place smaller kisses and nips along the edges of her mouth.

She told herself to stop, to wake up, to do something before she made a fool of herself. This couldn't be happening. She must have fallen asleep.

His tongue stroked the line between her lips, and she opened to him, letting him sink even deeper. For a dream, it felt all too real.

Bright lights danced behind her eyelids, and a fist of heat curled around her center. She wanted him to come even closer, to sink against her, to touch her all over. Fear of the consequences, and her embarrassment, had no power here.

Lullaby Lady let out a discordant crash of sound ending in a twang when Brian pulled back and one of his buttons hooked the low E.

Celia stared at him, stunned, shocked, and shaken to her core. It hadn't been a dream after all.

He laughed, clearly more comfortable than she'd ever been. "Next time, I'll have to remember to move the guitar first."

Her fingers crept up to bruised lips, skin sensitive where his dusting of evening shadow had scraped her. She glanced around, only then remembering Nick, who would be disturbed, or at least disgusted, by what they'd just done.

"He went to bed almost an hour ago. Too much pizza."

The blush slid up her neck until she felt overheated and faint.

Just how distracted had she been? Obviously too much to know what was going to happen.

Celia pushed to her feet and crossed to Lullaby Lady's case. She put the guitar away, knowing only that the lesson had ended, and she needed to get out of there. She thought she'd been so subtle. He only took what she'd offered blindly.

Brian's arms wrapped around her waist, the touch not at all similar to when he'd been the teacher.

The guitar dropped the last two inches, enough to jar the strings.

She ducked away from him. "Don't."

For once, Brian didn't condemn her treatment of the guitar. Instead, he stalked closer, his intent gaze making her back up until she met the unyielding wall.

"Why not? You want it as much as I do," he said, resting one hand on either side of her. "You were asking for me to touch you all night, even at dinner. I thought you weren't interested before, but now?"

Celia looked down, trying to avoid his stare. "I don't want... I didn't mean..." Though the words came from her mouth, they both knew her objections had no meaning. She had been contemplating just this and had failed to keep her interest to herself.

Brian jerked away, one hand slapping his side. "Is that it? You're some kind of tease? All tempt and no action?"

She stared at him for a moment, stunned at the accusation, then anger replaced embarrassment.

Celia pushed off the wall. Quick, angry strides took her to her jacket, and she shoved first one arm then the other into the sleeves.

"It's not appropriate," she told him. "You're my teacher. And there's Nick. And it's just not right."

Brian threw his head back to let out a laugh, but the humorless sound bit at her when she'd enjoyed his laughter before.

"Excuses. You're going to pretend you didn't lead me on? Stare at me with starry eyes and lick your lips. Even your nipples deny what you're saying."

Against her will, Celia glanced down to see two sharp points distorting the smooth line of her blouse. She pulled her jacket over to cover them. What could she say? How could she explain about her dreams without making this even worse? She had done everything he'd said, if not intentionally.

Part of her wanted to give in, but she knew she couldn't. He'd seen her invitation as simple lust. She wouldn't survive the aftermath, however much she longed to experience his touch for real. She'd had sex before, hard to be a runaway and avoid that situation, but this felt different. This time she cared.

"I think it's time for me to go home."

Her voice sounded small and quiet.

Brian thrust a hand through his hair, the fingers tangling the long strands. "Yeah, maybe you should. I won't apologize. I'm not sorry, and I don't think you really are either. But this isn't happening now. I get that. If ever it does, I want you to be willing—eager even. Not this. Better you go before we say something we'll both regret."

Celia nodded. She wanted to protest, to confirm he wasn't canceling her lessons as well, and knew Nick's disappointment made up only a small portion of her concern.

She said nothing.

"You can show yourself out. You know the way. Maybe by next Friday things will be different."

Turning before he could see her smile at the welcome reassurance, Celia crossed to the door. The sound of tuning started up behind her as soon as she moved into the hallway.

Celia hovered there for a moment before pulling herself away. She'd infringed on his privacy enough tonight without listening to him play when he thought he'd been left alone. In her darkest nightmares, she couldn't have imagined something worse than this. His angry words earlier chased her out of the house, louder for how they were at least partially deserved.

BRIAN LISTENED FOR THE DOOR, knowing he had acted like a hormonal teenager with no control. If he'd followed her out as much as he knew he shouldn't, he would have barred her path. Just because he'd been harboring lustful thoughts didn't mean she did. He had no right to push her. As to saying something they'd regret, well, his warning came too far behind the frustrated words.

After what seemed like an interminable time, the heavy front door swung closed.

He let out a sigh and finished tweaking Lullaby Lady's keys even though his fiddling had done more to put her out of tune than in.

What had happened there? Why had he reacted so violently? It was just a kiss…wasn't it?

He'd certainly kissed his share of women. This wasn't his first awkward relationship after all. He would never force himself on anyone. He didn't want to trespass where he wasn't welcomed wholeheartedly, especially not now. That she'd kissed him back at first didn't matter, though it hadn't helped his state one bit. Maybe he'd just gotten used to women jumping at the chance if he showed the least bit of interest, but part of the attraction with Celia had been how she didn't act like the other women he'd known.

Shifting on the chair did little to relieve the tension in his jeans, or his mind. Nor did adjusting the guitar so it rested against his thigh. If she hadn't stopped them, would they be sprawled on the floor right now, his hand tangled in her hair?

His fingers brushed the strings a little harder than they should have, but Lullaby Lady responded with a gamely burst of sound that reminded him of Celia. Her heart more than anything else. He still remembered the fierce concentration on her face as she tried to defend Nick. He thought her a busybody then, but it was before he'd come to know her.

A scatter of notes drifted from his fingers. Brian felt the swell of a song just waiting to spring to life. The words rose to his tongue, and he played with chording and picking to bring them together.

"She was just a complication. Too much for a simple man to bear."

He grinned. The line was all too clear, a little rough around the edges, but it held the truth.

So why had he kissed her? What had he been thinking? Had he been thinking at all?

Brian's lips sank into a frown, and he closed his eyes for a moment, seeking the absolution of dark. It didn't matter if she'd seemed willing, open, or even if she had been. He risked too much.

He enjoyed every minute spent in her company, enjoyed in a way sex could not replace, something he'd spent a lot of time and energy learning after Kaitlin sent him away. So much so even with harsh words between them, he'd made sure she would be coming back.

And Nick. He couldn't forget his son, his only responsibility. These lessons had brought the two of them together again. Would Nick have even wanted to try if not for Celia? What if she refused to return, too embarrassed or uncomfortable in his presence?

Losing her friendship, her connection with Nick, wasn't worth the momentary pleasure. Again his eyes slipped closed, but this time he didn't seek darkness. He drew on the memory instead.

Sensations flooded him, some he hadn't known he'd noticed.

The arc of her cheek, the way she tossed her short hair out of her face, how her lips didn't seem to thin when she smiled. Again, his fingers played along the fret board, but he knew he'd prefer to explore her ribcage, to run his fingers along the curve of her waist until his hands rested on her hips.

Brian laughed, a low, deep-throated sound. Had it been worth it? He hadn't felt so alive in more years than he could count. She made him feel this way. She caused this with her sweet blushes, her open laughter, and the dark shadows that sometimes clouded her eyes.

But her lips were temptation, the devil's work painted with an angel's hand.

He couldn't resist, he couldn't turn away. His fate to sink into her quicksand.

The notes came to him with an echo of her lips pressed to his, his fingers caressing the strings as if they were the curves of her body. Line after line, note after note, poured from him, the sardonic tone changing, slowing, smoothing into a tale of new beginnings, of chances thought lost and long forgotten.

Brian played it through again and again, tweaking a word, changing a major chord to minor, polishing and strengthening until he knew he had a hit on his hands. Sometimes the songs came with the assurance, the gut-level awareness this one had what it took to touch the hearts and souls of country music listeners everywhere.

His fingers stilled and then pressed flat on the strings, muting the last echo of sound.

Was that all he wanted from her? A song to wow his groupies? And when would he play the song anyway? He'd be a washed up has-been by the time Nick was old enough for Brian to head back on the road.

He stood up in one swift movement, his body wound tight with questions he couldn't answer or didn't want to. Lowering Lullaby Lady into her nest, he tried to push the frustration away. He wanted the new beginning, the hope that had crystallized in his song.

Brian laughed at himself even as he pulled out the notebook tucked into the inner pocket of Lullaby Lady's case. Celia hadn't known what a treasure she'd had. Those manuscript pages held all his early attempts at songwriting, things scratched down when he thought making it in the music industry was nothing more than a pipedream.

Somehow, recording her song there with his adolescent dreams seemed appropriate.

He dug in the pocket to retrieve the pencil, happy to find its tip still sharp enough. The real world sank away as he drew the notes and wrote the lyrics he'd hammered out and polished. Sometimes, he paused and sucked on the pencil tip, a bad habit he'd lost years ago, before changing a single word or adjusting a note.

Finally satisfied, Brian pulled the guitar out again. He crouched right there on the floor and played through the song, savoring each line. A few minor adjustments were required before he stored Lullaby Lady in her case.

Brian picked up the notebook and stared blindly out windows that already showed the touch of dawn. No matter how far he searched for a title, only one came to him, a title so simple, traditional, and right.

After licking the pencil tip once more, Brian printed in solid, dark letters: *Celia*.

Chapter 23

Brian lifted the heavy wood garage door, the one place in the house free of damage from the start. He used his car rarely, but he didn't know how this would go and didn't want to end up walking when he needed to get away quickly.

"Why can't I come, too?" Nick asked as he followed Brian, his voice just shy of a whine.

Thrusting a hand through his hair, Brian turned to look at his son. He didn't want to admit what he'd done to Nick any more than he wanted to face Celia, and he definitely didn't want Nick there when he did. Who knew how the meeting would go?

"You're going to see her, aren't you? Is it a date? Are you going to get married?"

That startled a chuckle out of Brian when he'd thought himself too tense to laugh. "No, not a date. I said—did— something stupid. It's an apology."

Nick gave him a solemn look and nodded with an understanding more mature than his years. "You should bring her flowers. It's what my dad always did."

The words hit Brian like a punch in the gut. Of course Nick would consider Kaitlin's second husband his father. He barely remembered Brian. A twisted happiness rose at the proof Kaitlin's second attempt at marriage hadn't been perfect, but Brian let it float away without dwelling. He'd loved Kaitlin a long time ago, and part of him always would, but he'd moved on.

He rested a hand on the hood of his Mustang, one of the few things he'd kept from his old life. "I don't think flowers will cut it this time."

"That bad? She's still coming on Friday, isn't she?"

Brian blew out a breath as he searched for somewhere between truth and his fears. "I hope so, Nick. I really do."

Nick smiled when Brian expected a frown. "You should get her a new guitar to practice with. Then, she'll have to come if she wants to get good at it. To do it justice. You tell me so all the time."

Brian considered the idea and could see its merit. He'd planned an apology, but she could accept it and still cut ties. Besides, what better way to show he meant it than to bring her further into his world?

Relaxing for the first time since the decision to catch her at the bookstore, Brian reached out and rubbed Nick's head. "Sounds like a better plan than any I could think up. Don't worry. She won't be able to risk claiming her own Lullaby Lady."

"Celia, there's someone here for you."

Celia ran a tired hand across her face and tucked the last magazine onto the shelf. Some kids had taken every single magazine out and put them back in a big jumble, making this the worst week ever. Whoever had asked for her, she hoped they wouldn't take long. A glance at her watch showed her shift ended five minutes ago.

"Coming," she said, trying to infuse her voice with cheerful enthusiasm, an attempt that was no more successful this time than it had been any of the other ones today.

Already Wednesday, and Friday loomed close. She hadn't stopped dreaming of Brian, either. Now her nights began with a long stretch of castigating herself and trying to figure out how she could avoid acting like a fool, only to have her subconscious mind take over the minute she fell asleep.

She reached the end of the book stacks and glanced up, looking for the customer. Instead, her gaze tripped over Melanie's grin.

Her gut clenched, foreboding sweeping through her before she turned to face the man at her coworker's side. At first, the suit confused her, but it was none other than Brian.

He'd cleaned up nicely and done something to trap his hair so it looked like a normal length. He wore a dark blue pinstripe, a tie snug against his neck. She could see a flash of the businessman he'd once been, and she didn't like it. Celia wanted her Brian back.

"Hi," he said, his tone soft.

All at once, what he wore didn't matter. The desires she'd been resisting crashed over her. She stared at him, unsure what to say.

"Aren't you going to say hi, too?" Melanie asked with a teasing chuckle.

Celia shook her head, returning to awareness when the world had narrowed to just the two of them a moment before.

"Hi." Her answer came out terse, and she added a nod to seal the tone. "I'm done with my shift. Melanie can help you."

Without giving him the chance to respond, she turned and headed for the back to collect her purse and jacket. Behind her, Melanie let out a surprised exclamation, but Celia didn't stop until a hand caught her arm and Brian stepped in front of her.

"I didn't come for books," he said, a hint of frustration in his tone. He sighed, then frowned. "Look, I know Friday went a little sideways at the end. I wanted to apologize. To make sure everything's alright between us."

Celia pulled free and shook her head. "There is no us."

A surprised snort from Melanie made Celia aware of her surroundings once again. It seemed criminal how easily Brian could draw her into another world.

She gave him a frown of her own. "Let me get my things." Though she still didn't trust herself with him, they weren't going to discuss the issue in front of Melanie if she could help it.

The few minutes of respite strengthened her resolve to keep this meeting quick and painless. If she was to have any chance of surviving Friday, she needed to build up some walls between them. She needed time.

Brian waited outside the employees-only door, looking as if he hadn't moved at all. "You ready then?"

"Come on," Celia answered, jerking her head toward the main entrance. Whatever he thought she would be ready for, he'd learn differently soon enough.

As though aware of her mood, Brian respected her silence all the way through the shop. Celia still couldn't think of a thing to say, though, once they were out on the street. Habit started her walking home, and he fell into step beside her. She almost protested, but then she could still linger at Mr. Peterson's shop if he hadn't broken off.

A hand on her shoulder jerked her to a stop.

"What?" Celia demanded, angry now at the way he seemed to shove her around.

"This is it. My car."

She glanced at the blue muscle car parked at the curb, startled. Celia walked everywhere and had begun to like the quiet without the thrum of engines. Now, it seemed a perfect opportunity to get rid of Brian before she said or did something foolish, something that would end up with both of them frustrated and unhappy instead of just her.

"Oh, right then. Goodbye." The words rushed out as she tugged at his hold, attempting to continue her walk.

"It's too far to walk. We'll need to drive." He opened the door with his free hand and waved at her to get in.

Celia glanced inside, half expecting to find Nick tucked in the back seat.

The car was empty.

"I don't know about you, but I'm heading home. It's not too far to walk any other day of the week." Confusion vied with annoyance, and both showed in her tone.

He gave a startled laugh. "Look, let's start again. I meant to suggest I take you to the music store. You still need to get a guitar, and I want you to choose a decent one." He waved at the car again. "I thought if I came along, I could help you out. Make sure you don't end up with some warped-neck trash can."

Celia turned to look him in the face, reading there what his tone hinted at. He meant this as some kind of penance for his behavior on Friday. Only she knew she'd been at least as much of the problem as he had.

"Please?"

He said nothing more, even letting go of her arm and stepping back so the decision was hers alone to make. Celia hesitated for a moment longer, but gave in. She couldn't hold him accountable for something not entirely his fault. She was tortured enough by what almost happened for both of them.

Besides, as much as she knew the dangers of spending more time with him, especially alone, she couldn't deny the part of her that thrilled to the thought of hours in his presence.

"Alright, I'll come," Celia said as she slid into the low, lounge chair of a seat. "Thank you." The last she added in an attempt to soften what might have seemed a grudging consent. And with the decision behind her, excitement grew at the thought of having her own Lullaby Lady, of someday being able to make music with even a fraction of Brian's skill.

Nestled in the bucket seat with the engine's deep rumble making conversation difficult, she let her mind drift into daydreams of the two of them playing music together.

Chapter 24

Brian glanced over at Celia, but she was leaning back with her head turned to look out the window. She'd been so quiet the whole trip. He wished he could read her mind. He wanted to understand why she'd decided to go after all.

Was it just to have his help choosing a guitar or did she want to forgive him?

He grimaced and stared out the windshield. His questions were classic for elementary school. Does she like me? Or is she just using me to get to the cookies Mom packed in my lunchbox? The craving to know the answer didn't feel any different, but the rules were much more complicated.

The song he'd written about her haunted him until he couldn't last another day without seeing if he'd imagined the connection between them. He'd needed to apologize anyway, and Nick's suggestion felt perfect when they'd discussed it in the garage. Now, though, he couldn't tell whether she came along because she wanted a guitar or shared the same urge to spend time with him.

"We're almost there," Brian said to break the silence.

Celia glanced over at him. "Oh. I've never been to this side of town."

He laughed once. "I wish I could be a tour guide, but I found this shop in the phone book."

There had been more than one instrument shop, which had surprised him for a small town like Foster's Way. He'd chosen this one out of the three options not because it specialized in guitars but the opposite. The Treble Clef focused on orchestral instruments. He hoped they'd be just as likely to have quality guitars, and with a more classical focus, the staff might not recognize him. Especially since he'd chosen to wear the suit he'd bought in case he needed to go to court to claim Nick. It wasn't anything like what he'd worn in his old life, or new. They said the clothes made the man. He hoped the suit would at least keep him anonymous.

Celia turned to look out the window again.

He thought she'd ended the short conversation, but as they passed a stretch of restaurants and what looked like clubs, she murmured, "Melanie, the young woman you met at the bookstore, is always trying to get me to come down here. They have some decent talent, according to her. No big names, but some folks able to carry a tune."

"But?" he said after the silence stretched out again.

She laughed. "Oh, nothing really. I just remembered how she said they did open mic nights where anyone could go try their hand. I was thinking of doing that someday when I thought Lullaby Lady was going to be mine."

Brian swung his car into an open parking space and eyed the vehicles on either side. At least they were both well maintained. He didn't want either yellow or red marks on his car.

Celia pushed on her door, and he flinched, expecting the sound of contact, but she caught the swing before it could connect with the other vehicle.

He gave her a smile she didn't see, grateful for whoever had taught her the right way to get out, especially since she didn't drive.

She laughed, catching the edge of his expression after all. "In the city, if you bump a car, you could set off enough noise to wake the dead."

He'd forgotten she came from the big city. She didn't talk about it—or seem to miss it—much at all.

Brian put an arm around her shoulders, half expecting her to object, but she neither pulled away nor leaned in as he steered her toward the door. "It's this way."

He thought she would laugh at the store's name, but then wondered if she understood it. This might have been a bad idea. He didn't want her intimidated.

She reached for the handle and pulled the door open before he could change his mind. They stepped inside to the melodic chime of hand bells.

The space they entered seemed huge compared to the stores in his hometown, but then rent would be lower out here. Brian scanned the room, glancing past violins, wind instruments, and even a few full-sized orchestral basses. He breathed out in relief when he spotted a wall in the back decorated with a variety of guitars.

The slender man behind the counter glanced up from some paperwork and waved. "I'll be right with you folks. Feel free to look around."

Celia leaned close and pushed up on her toes to whisper, "I really can't spend all that much on this."

Brian laughed. "Don't worry. I'm sure they have ones in many price ranges. And there are good guitars in every category. You just have to be willing to take the time to find the right one."

"Oh. Okay."

From the grateful look she tossed him, he could tell she appreciated his presence here at least. If he had his way, though, she'd come to see him as more than just a source of music knowledge.

Celia walked over to where acoustics hung in two rows, the more expensive ones displayed out of reach. Brian watched how she stroked each one then checked the price tag, unwilling to fall for a guitar out of her range.

He loved the strange mix of mystic and practical he found in Celia. Like the way she'd played with Nick in the park. Most adults wouldn't take the time, or go down to the park in the first place on the offhand chance of finding someone interested in a game. But Celia would.

And not just once, either.

The way she held Lullaby Lady, and the way she hadn't laughed at the guitar's name, offered further insight into her character.

All those parts of her drew him, but at the same time, she'd proved herself to be practical. She wouldn't commit where she didn't have the resources.

If only he had the smarts to do the same.

Celia should have been off limits. He didn't want to sour her relationship with Nick any more than he wanted her turning away from him. If he'd been lonely, he should have chosen a better partner. One without so much risk.

"She's a real catch, your wife."

Brian started, turning to find the clerk eyeing Celia just as he had been.

For a heartbeat, he wanted to shove the man away, wanted to lay claim to her as his woman, not for others to admire. Then he twisted his lips into a smile and found himself agreeing without bothering to correct the man's assumption. He had no idea how Celia would react if he acted all possessive, but he wasn't above pretending the relationship for a while.

"Yeah, she sure is something special."

"Just look at her. She doesn't know a thing about what she's doing, but she's searching for the connection, you know."

Brian twisted to stare at the guy, his eyebrows raised. Here he'd thought the man admired her looks, but the clerk had seen the same thing that caught Brian's attention.

"That's why I'm here. To make sure she makes the right choice."

The clerk shook his thatch of blond hair and grinned. "We wouldn't want her choosing something out of her league like a high-end Ovation. It would be too much of a waste."

Brian nodded in agreement without even thinking about it. This man knew his business. He saw something more than just wood. Nor could he deny the man's logic. Lullaby Lady had come from the lower end as well. There was no point in starting out with an expensive guitar. That waited until Celia proved she would stick it out.

He stifled a laugh at the thought.

Celia wasn't the type to jump into something half-hearted. She'd already had the goal of playing an open mic night before she knew three basic chords. She wouldn't give up, something he had every reason to be grateful for.

As long as she held on to the dream, he had the excuse to see her, to convince her, despite his clumsy approach last week, he wanted to be friends. More could come later. He'd learn patience if it killed him.

"Can I look at this one?" Celia called from the other side of the room.

"Sure," the man said. "You going to take them down for her, or do you need help?" he added, looking at Brian.

Brian accepted the man's confidence without thinking, then wondered if he'd recognized Brian after all. There didn't seem to be awareness in the man's open expression, though, so maybe he just recognized experience.

He crossed the room, his gaze on Celia the whole time, and thoughts of the clerk faded. Instead, the assumption they were married took hold.

He could imagine Celia as his wife, though his mind hadn't moved in that direction since Kaitlin. They could play guitar together in the evenings, play checkers with Nick, then cuddle on the soft, cushioned sofa he'd get for the parlor. They could walk down to the park, maybe even get a dog, and sip brandy before the fire. After he got the chimney cleaned out, of course. He could tuck her against his side and they'd go upstairs...

"Are you going to get it down, or does the clerk have to?"

Brian returned to the present with a thump to see Celia staring at him with an odd expression. She licked her lips as though nervous, and he wanted to taste the moisture her tongue had left behind more than anything.

Did she mean to provoke him? Or was he so absorbed in his own desires, he assumed she felt the same.

"The guitar?"

"Right."

He told himself to focus as he brought down one guitar after another. He tried not to think of his own arm in place of the curved body as she leaned forward, her small breasts pressing into unyielding wood.

"What about this one?"

At her question, he felt a flush heat his neck. "Strum the strings again, one note at a time. No, don't chord, just open strings." The underlying buzz vanished when she lifted her fingers, and the sound came through clean. "It's got high action, higher than Lullaby Lady, but you can get used to that. You just have to press harder. How does it feel?"

Celia glanced up at him, and a smile brightened her whole face. "Like she's mine."

Brian laughed. "Then the guitar should be."

The clerk had been keeping out of sight, but clearly paying attention as he came forward to help them. He handled the purchase smoothly and with elegance. He didn't try to cheat or trick her, but Celia walked out with a guitar, a soft case, extra strings, and a tuner.

Her grin never faltered, even when she paid out more, probably, than she'd been expecting.

"And don't forget to stop by for any supplies you need. I've got it all," the man said. "I sure hope your wife enjoys her guitar."

"But—"

Brian grabbed her arm, swept up the guitar case, and tugged her out the door before she could correct the man. He wanted to hold on to the idea, to know someone believed they belonged together even if she didn't. If he thought about it long enough, he'd have to admit how ridiculous the idea was. So he didn't let himself think.

Chapter 25

"Ha, I knew he reminded me of someone."

Celia jolted hard enough to send the pile of paperbacks she'd been filing scattering across the floor. "Melanie, you scared me." Though her voice still shook, she softened her words with a smile. Her coworker couldn't know she'd had hardly any sleep. She'd spent the night practicing and learning her new instrument when she wasn't daydreaming about Brian. He'd cared enough to apologize, to help her choose a guitar yesterday. Maybe they had a chance at something more after all.

"Oh, sorry." Melanie crouched down to help restore order, pulling Celia from her thoughts. "It's just something's been nagging me ever since your boyfriend came to pick you up yesterday."

"He's not my boyfriend," Celia said for not the first time.

"Whatever. If he's not, he certainly wants to be. I'm a good judge of that kind of thing."

Celia felt heat rush up her neck even as she shook her head. "It's not like that. I'm a friend of his son's."

"You mean they make two of them? Can I have the older model then?"

A laugh burst out of Celia, and her hand collided with Melanie's as she reached for a book without looking. "He's my guitar teacher. His son is twelve, remember, and my teacher's probably half again your age. I don't think there's much of a future for you in either direction."

Melanie frowned for a moment as she absorbed the information, then shrugged. "Just means the dad's perfect for you. I get your fascination with country now."

Celia shot her coworker a confused look.

She didn't know how to feel about Melanie's prying. She'd always kept her private life private. Well, what little of one she'd had.

"Anyway, the suit threw me off for a while, but then I remembered where I'd seen his face."

The books all collected and in alphabetical order, Celia went back to stocking, only giving Melanie half her attention. "Hmm?" Celia let the sound carry whatever interpretation Melanie needed, focused instead on shuffling one shelf over to make room.

"Well, your boyfriend—not boyfriend—is the spitting image of the missing country singer. Now I understand the gossip saying he's hiding out right here in Foster's Way. I thought it was him at first, but that can't be right. I mean, no big, award-winning, hit singer's going to come to Foster's Way, but if people saw your guy?"

Celia rolled onto her heels, and the book slipped from her hand to thud against the floor. She barely heard it. The radio had made some mention of a missing singer, but she'd paid no attention. It hadn't mattered then.

Suddenly, it mattered a lot.

Melanie was so wrong in her assumptions. Someone famous would come to a place like Foster's Way to hide. A place where he'd find people like her who didn't know enough to recognize a star, people he could dupe into thinking he was some desperate father down on his luck trying to make good for his son. All those funny looks when he'd told her his name now made sense. At least he hadn't lied about that.

Her hands clenched into fists, though she wouldn't have considered herself a violent person.

Had he laughed with Nick whenever she brought over pizza? Did they normally have catered meals with everything provided, even down to the plates and silverware? And all his talk about the house. She'd been foolish enough to think he'd done the work with his own hands. Proud of him for it.

"Hey, are you alright? You're not looking too good."

Celia dragged in a slow breath, trying to chase away the icy chill that had taken over her body. Her hands trembled, and she'd never felt so cold. Why did she care so much? It wasn't as if they were dating or anything. He was her teacher. No more. Wasn't he?

She needed to know for sure, to see for herself. "Melanie, Show me a picture, an article or something. I have to know."

Melanie stared back at her with wide eyes as though stunned by her urgency. Then a look of horror crossed the girl's face.

"Oh no. You mean it really is him? And he didn't tell you? That's bad, Celia, really bad."

Celia managed a shaky laugh. "You could be wrong. Maybe he just vaguely resembles this other guy." She kept to herself all the times she'd thought he should be playing for an audience much bigger than two, how she'd wanted to bring some music magnate in to hear him.

Dressed as he was, Melanie probably thought he'd come from the city to see her at first, but with this, she'd been quick enough to connect the country music with Brian.

Melanie pushed to her feet and grabbed Celia's arm to pull her up as well. "I'm usually pretty on target about things like this, but it's easy enough to check. Come on."

She dragged Celia over to the magazine racks they'd reorganized only yesterday when Celia's head had been in the clouds and her mind too filled with thoughts of Brian to do more than glance at the titles.

"Here."

Celia lifted her hands to accept a copy of *The New Country Weekly*, its title familiar from her organizing. She didn't remember the rest of the cover, but she did recognize it. There, splashed on the front for everyone to see, stood her derelict, her fallen man, the one she'd come to love. Her heart twisted into a knot.

She didn't love him; she couldn't.

Celia sank to the floor, her gaze fixed on the image while her life shattered into layers of deceit. How could she love someone who had lied to her from their very first meeting? He wasn't who she'd thought he was at all.

Numb, her glance wandered over the words without comprehension until they reached the teaser printed in bright white letters across Brian's feet:

Where is Brian Lakes? And how could he abandon his adoring public?

As if pounding in the nails of her coffin, the letters slammed into her head. Brian Lakes. He hadn't even bothered to keep his name from her. Why should he have? It was common enough. Even if she had known about the singer, she wouldn't have believed it without this damning picture. Like Melanie said, why would he have come here?

Her fingers moved mechanically, flipping the pages until she found the rest of the story. Nick warranted a tiny mention, but most of the spread was devoted to Brian's ex-wife, his dead ex-wife. The one he'd loved with his heart and soul, leaving nothing left for all the other women who had tried to catch him after the divorce.

Celia wanted to crumple up the magazine and throw it as far from her as she could and scream at the top of her lungs. What had she been to him then? Why had he kissed her?

Of course he'd called her a tease. What she'd hoped was more had only been lust. He didn't have a heart to offer, and even if he did, he wasn't interested in offering it to her. At least she'd stopped them from going any further. He might think nothing of falling into bed with any willing female, but Celia hadn't wanted that for years.

Melanie tugged the magazine from Celia's clenched fingers and smoothed the pages. "Another minute in your hands, and it would have to come out of your pay," she said, her face concerned even if her tone was joking.

Celia forced a smile and ignored the tripping of her heartbeat. "It's a bit of a shock, but it wasn't like he meant anything to me. I told you he isn't my boyfriend."

Melanie pulled Celia into her arms for a hug. "You keep telling yourself that, and it'll start feeling true. Don't let him get you down. He wasn't just hiding from you; he's hiding from everyone."

Then, the girl leaned back and stared at Celia with a wicked grin on her face. "I know just the thing for payback. There's a number in the magazine article. A tip line. Give him up. He lied to you. Expose his lie to the world."

For just a heartbeat, the idea called to Celia's darker nature. Trust had never been easy, not since the day she ran away from home.

Then Nick surged into her thoughts, and she shook her head. "I can't. It's complicated. He wouldn't be the only one hurt. Melanie, you can't say anything. You can't tell anyone about this."

"You're just going to let him get away with it?" Melanie looked as incredulous as she sounded.

Celia shook her head slowly. "No. I can't pretend I don't know, but I'll deal with it my own way." She squared her shoulders and pushed the hurt down. "But for now, we better get back to work. What if a customer had come in?"

Melanie slapped her gently on the shoulder. "That's my girl. Strong and collected. He's going to regret ever trying to play games with you."

BRIAN PUTTERED ABOUT THE KITCHEN, too distracted to focus on anything. Catalogs lay scattered across the tabletop, but whenever he looked at the selection of couches, tables, chairs, rugs, or anything, his thoughts drifted to Celia.

He could imagine her here, helping him decide, cuddling with him on one sofa or another, and making this place her own. Those thoughts only made him want her here now; he wanted the music shop clerk's assumption to be true.

He slapped the counter and scowled at the cabinets that usually inspired joy. He had no idea how to approach her, no idea if she was interested in him as a man. Returning his kiss might have been instinct. She'd certainly been quick enough to try to correct the man's error and to pull away from Brian.

His first guitar gig, he'd been sixteen, barely old enough to date, much less understand women. From that moment on, he'd never met someone who didn't know who he was. Even his parents' friends had heard of his growing fame. His parents convinced him to finish high school before accepting a contract and diving head first into the music world. As soon as the ink dried on his high school diploma, though, he'd been out the door.

Something simple as sticking out his hand and saying his name had been alien when he came here. He'd chosen such an out of the way place in the hopes no one would know him, or care if they did recognize the country star. Then, he'd spent most of his time hiding out, afraid his cover would be blown.

Everyone he'd met since breaking out wanted something; he'd understood that, and accepted them because of it. Clear motivations.

What did Celia see in him though? She didn't want something from him, or at least not the same somethings he'd known: a quick tumble, a signature smeared in lipstick above a low-cut concert t-shirt, a job on the crew, or an introduction to his agent. Those things he could wrap his mind around. But she didn't know about the music scene.

Even though she'd pulled away from his kiss last Friday, she'd seemed embarrassed, not repulsed. And she'd been the one to look at him with desire in her eyes, a longing he'd thought he'd understood. Brian had never lacked for confidence.

He'd been raised in a good family, encouraged at every turn, and though he hadn't realized it before, been given anything he desired.

Only Kaitlin had bucked the trend.

A sweep of his hand sent the catalogs fluttering to the floor. Brian clenched his fingers over the back of one of the kitchen chairs until the wood creaked.

How could Celia be interested in this? What did she see when she looked at him and his ramshackle, unfurnished house? She'd come here first for Nick. Had she stayed for the same reason?

He closed his eyes, and her face, glowing with happiness, painted itself on his eyelids. He'd wanted so much to drop a kiss onto her full lower lip when she'd declared the guitar her own. He'd wanted to claim her right then, right there, not caring who saw them.

But why would she want to connect her life to his? What did he have to offer her? Or rather, what did she think he did?

A violent shake of his head sent the strands of hair away from his face, but then they sank over his eyes again. If he wanted to start something with her, if he was serious about all this, he'd have to trust her with his secret. He'd have to chance everything he was building here for himself, for Nick, and even for her.

"What would she say if I did? What would she believe?"

"Believe what?" Nick popped through the door, startling Brian. The boy glanced around and shook his head, a grin plastered across his face. "You sure made a mess in here. You need to clean it up, or Brian is going to tell you off."

Brian laughed, pushing away the tension of unanswerable questions in favor of enjoying his son. "Brian's a real tough cookie, isn't he? Wouldn't want to get on his bad side."

Nick laughed too. "That's right. It's not a good idea. I'll help you clean up here, if you'll make something for lunch. He's better when fed."

"You mean you are."

A glance to the clock showed more time had passed than Brian expected while he'd daydreamed about Celia and the impossible task in front of him. Could he put his happiness before Nick's? He had no way of knowing if Celia would help them keep his anonymity here.

Nick had already started picking up the catalogs, and Brian bent to help.

"What would you think if Celia came around here more often?" The question slipped out before he could stop it.

His son stood up to dump the pile of catalogs onto the table. "What? Like for more lessons?"

Before Brian could correct the assumption, Nick's face took on a sly look. "Or do you mean like dating?"

A flush heated the back of Brian's neck, and he felt as awkward as a teenager introducing the concept of dating to his own father. "Yeah, something like that. Would you mind?"

Nick considered for a moment, then shook his head. "I like her."

Apparently, it was enough. Enough of an answer, and enough of the conversation.

They moved on to other topics, folded down the corners of some pages with reasonable furniture, and shared a lunch of cold cut sandwiches.

It didn't take much of a stretch to see Celia comfortable and happy here with them. She seemed to fit in wherever they did.

Chapter 26

Thursday finally drew to a close, and Celia felt lucky she hadn't been fired with all the stupid errors she'd made and the sharp comments to customers. Melanie shot her a sympathetic look, but her coworker's understanding only made things worse.

Brian's betrayal ate at her. It soured the joy she'd found in her new guitar, curdled any good feelings she'd had toward the man, and changed her dread about the next lesson into something very different. She'd told Melanie she could handle this on her own, and she would. If only she could think of how.

"Go on home and rest a bit. My mom always said things look better in the morning."

Celia laughed, the bitterness in the sound surprising her. "Somehow, I don't think he could look better in the morning, or any other time. I can't get past the feeling I was just some kind of dumb groupie to him."

Melanie shook her head. "From the sound of it, you weren't anything, and I'd say that was your choice, not his. Maybe he has a good reason."

"Are you trying to make me feel better? He only thought of me as a groupie rather than getting to treat me as one?" Celia snatched up her purse but the strap hooked the edge of the box where it had been resting. The flap fell open to reveal even more copies of the hated magazine.

She leaned closer and scowled.

No, this was another title. How could she have been so stupid? How could she not have noticed with all this publicity, and how could he have thought he'd get away with it?

Celia pushed aside the memory of how she'd forced her way into his dilapidated castle, not the other way round. He should have been honest with her, not let her think he was down on his luck. He shouldn't have let her feel sorry for him.

She picked up the top magazine, wishing she still only felt pity for Brian. "I'm going to confront him with this. That's what I'm going to do." Some of her restless anger eased now that she had a plan, a purpose.

"I'll shove the magazine under his nose and see how he tries to wriggle his way out of this."

Melanie gently took the magazine from her hands. "Sounds like a good plan, but how about taking one of the issues out there. This one isn't supposed to go on the shelves until Sunday."

Celia looked at the girl blankly for a moment, then glanced at the box to see the open by date.

"Figures," she muttered. "But why is he such big news all of a sudden? He must have been gone for a couple of months at least."

Melanie scanned the cover. "Says here there are rumors one of his songs will be nominated for a Country Music Award. That's enough to bring his name back into the limelight."

"His name, his picture, but not him." Celia shrugged. "Maybe he doesn't know yet. I can deliver the happy news…on the end of a sharp stick."

She swept out of the employee-only area, selected a magazine, and called goodbye to Melanie. Melanie would ring her up and handle the payment. She wanted to get this over with before she lost her nerve.

The walk didn't calm her temper, but the familiar sight of his house brought forth memories of the fun times they'd shared, of him teaching her music, of listening to his beautiful voice, even of endless checkers games and takeout pizza. She faltered, wishing somehow she could forget what she'd learned and things could go back to what they had been.

Her gaze fell to the sidewalk, but not before it brushed the magazine still clutched in her hand.

No, she wasn't that much of a coward. She couldn't live in a land of pretend, not now when she was finally learning how to create a life of her own.

Before she could mount the steps, though, the door swung open, and Brian and Nick appeared at the top.

"Hi, Celia," Nick called when he saw her. "You coming to the park with us?"

Celia's gaze jerked to Brian and hung there, captured.

"I wasn't expecting you today," he said, his voice husky.

A shiver ran down her spine, a visceral connection tying her to this man and none other.

"Nick, you go on ahead. I have something to tell Celia."

The boy looked disappointed for a moment, then grinned. "Okay. I'll see you later, Celia."

She felt struck dumb as Nick slipped past her and scampered off to the park, leaving her alone with his father.

Brian walked down, slipped an arm around her waist, and pulled her unresisting into his house. Whatever anger had sustained her seemed gone, lost in his gaze. Even the touch of glossy paper against her fingers on the opposite side from Brian couldn't call it back.

The door swung shut behind them, and he turned to face her. "I'm glad you came. I have something I want to tell you."

All at once, she didn't want to hear it. She refused to face another lie, another trap to suck her in. She raised her arm and pushed the magazine toward him, exhaustion, not anger the driving force.

"Here," was all she could manage.

"Well, we could go to the kitchen. It's more comforta—"

She could tell the moment he saw what she offered, understood what she meant. Celia looked for the daunting guilt, but instead, his features darkened into anger.

"I should have known," Brian said, grinding the words out through clenched teeth. "You were just softening me up before coming in for the kill. I don't matter. Nick doesn't matter. Just some signature to sell."

He grabbed the magazine from her and plucked a pen from a nearby cup. The hallway table holding the cup hadn't been there last week, an improvement she would have found encouraging yesterday.

"This is what you really want," he said, scrawling his name across the cover. "All your ignorant innocence, the way you didn't react to my name, it was a game to you, wasn't it? Just play acting. You only wanted to get close—to get under my skin."

He shoved the signed copy at her, slammed the pen into the cup, and strode away, deeper into the house.

Over his shoulder, he tossed, "Well, it didn't work. You can just leave now. Leave and never come back."

Celia stared after him, flinching when the kitchen door slammed. Whatever she'd expected, it hadn't been this. She'd been betrayed here, not him. How dare he?

Without a conscious decision, she found herself stomping down the hallway and slamming the kitchen door open hard enough so it smacked into the wall.

"I don't want your stupid signature," she shouted, throwing the magazine down on the table in front of him. "I couldn't care less that you're famous. To me, you are just a stinking liar. You let me believe— You led me on. You're— You're— There aren't words bad enough for what you are."

She stood there for a moment, too caught up in her anger to say anything more, fighting back the boiling curse words she'd learned from her street kids. She wanted to hit him, to hurt him as badly as he'd hurt her, she wanted to throw something, to break something, to— She didn't know what she wanted.

Brian's stare seemed to pierce her anger, to bore its way into her until Celia could not ignore it. She shifted, desperately clutching for the determination she'd felt only a moment before.

"Do you mean it?"

His simple words freed her, and with a wave of renewed anger, she slammed her hands onto his chest.

"Of course I mean it. You are the scum of the earth. You lied to me, not once, not a small lie, but every single time with every single word out of your mouth."

His chair scraped back from the table, and he grabbed her hands before she could move away. "You really didn't know? You really don't care?"

Celia shook her head, the questions making no sense. "Just let me go." Her voice came out quiet, almost a whisper. "I'm done. I can't do this anymore." If she'd had a free hand, she would have rubbed the ache over her heart, a sensation more emotional than physical for once.

He dropped to his knees, still holding her hands trapped. "Can't do what?"

She jerked on his hold, but her hands wouldn't come free. "You want your pound of flesh, is that it? You can't let me go until you've won this little game?" Though she tried to stay angry, her words just sounded tired and bitter. "I can't stay here. I can't be here with you, knowing it was all a lie, knowing the man I fell in love with never existed."

Suddenly, her hands were free, but the rest of her soon wasn't. Brian's joyful shout rang in her ears as he jumped up and tugged her tight against him.

"I'm sorry," he whispered into her hair. "I'm sorry I didn't tell you. No one was supposed to know. I had to keep the media away just until Nick and I learned how to live with each other. I wasn't hiding from you; I wasn't trying to make a fool of you. You weren't supposed to be here at all."

It was the last that penetrated Celia's numb state, the last sentence spoken with such frustration, such confusion, it left no room for doubt.

She pushed him away, wanting to see his face, but even so, she regretted when he let her slide to the ground and released her.

He stepped back and turned, resting both hands on the counter. "I suppose it doesn't matter why. I understand your anger. I even shared it once. Betrayal lingers. I've really blown it this time."

Celia crossed to him in two quick strides and wrapped her arms around his middle, resting her head on his spine.

"You didn't betray me," she whispered, only now realizing the truth. "You didn't tell me about your career, but I didn't ask either. I thought I had it all figured out. But you didn't hold yourself back either. I've seen into the heart of you. I've seen the truth of your love for Nick, your frustrations, your anger. I know you. Maybe not the star, but I know you."

She tugged his arm until he turned to face her. "I've seen the real man, the one who doesn't spend his time on glossy magazine covers, and that's the Brian I want."

A stunned look appeared on his face for a moment before joy swept it away. Again he picked her up, but this time he pressed her lips to his, and she returned the touch with equal fervor. There would be no pulling away.

When they finally broke apart, both were breathless.

Celia laughed and stroked his cheek with one hand, loving the feel of his rough skin, loving him.

"I love you, Celia. And I want to tell you everything so nothing stands between us."

Celia glanced down to where his supporting arm still pressed her tight to his lean form.

"Nothing stands between us now."

He opened his mouth, but she pressed a finger to it. "I understand. And I want to hear everything about you I don't already know. But it won't change anything. Not anything in here"—she touched her head—"or here"—she touched her heart. "Even when I found out your secret, I still loved you. I didn't want to, but I did."

Brian stared down at her, his eyes saying what his mouth could not.

She pushed up on tiptoe to kiss him one more time, then stepped away, her whole body warm with his touch. "Right now, though, there's a great kid waiting for us at the park."

Brian's smile widened into a grin and he looked happier than she had ever seen him. "I can tell you on the way. It's times like these I wish I'd sprung for a cell phone for Nick. Of course, if I hadn't chased him down there that first time, I'd never have met you."

Celia linked her arm through his. "You forget. I had your guitar. We were destined to come together."

Brian paused at the kitchen table, and when she saw why, Celia wanted to protest, but he shook his head. "You might as well keep it. My signature is worth something on eBay."

She accepted the magazine and jammed it into the top of her purse. Whether he'd been joking or not, she would never sell it. If nothing else, the magazine stood as a reminder to ask before letting anger take hold. Someday, it might come in handy as they weathered the storms of a real relationship.

Epilogue

Nick bounced in the back seat with Sunsinger strapped into the seat next to him. Celia's tension grew with every minute. "I can't believe you talked me into this. I'm not ready. I've only had my guitar for a few weeks, and your lessons not much longer."

Brian glanced over, his expression full of pride and love. "You've practiced the song backwards and forwards. You know it by heart. You can do this. Sunsinger is dying for a chance to show off her stuff."

Celia gave him a tight smile, but his confidence only made her feel worse. Knowing what she did, how could she stand having him and Nick watch her perform up on stage? No matter how much she'd practiced, even if the crowd didn't scare her silly, she couldn't hope to match Brian's talent. Even before she discovered his true identity, she'd known how much music meant to him.

Her stomach churned, and she wanted nothing more than to turn back and hide out in her little cottage.

"You don't have to play," Brian said in a low voice. "Not if you really don't want to. We can just listen tonight. Or we can head back, make sure Nick's in bed on time, and watch a movie or something."

Celia turned to stare at him, amazed once again at how easily he could read her moods and understand her thoughts.

He pulled to a stop at a light and ran a hand along her thigh, the touch soothing and exciting all at once.

Images filled her mind of time spent on Brian's new sofa, one he'd asked her to help choose on the assumption she'd be using it as much as any of them. He made her feel warm, comfortable, safe, and desired. He made her feel like part of the family, something she'd never really had.

Her shoulders straightened, and she stared out the windshield into the gathering darkness. He could give her a lot of things, but courage came from within. She'd spent enough of life hiding first literally then behind her work. She'd moved to Foster's Way for a new beginning. That wouldn't happen if she shrank from the challenge.

"No. I don't want to go back. I want to do this. I've practiced enough. We both know it. And I refuse to be some shrinking violet unwilling to live life to the fullest."

His hand squeezed her upper thigh once before he moved it to the stick shift as the light changed.

"Somehow, I knew you'd feel that way," Brian said, sending her a laughing glance.

She repaid his arrogance by running her fingers along his inner thigh and watching the flush creep up his neck. Comfort hadn't been the only emotion they'd shared on the sofa.

"And we'll be right there cheering for you," came Nick's voice, a necessary reminder of where they were, and with whom.

"But you better sit down, Nick. Your seatbelt can't help you if you prevent it from working."

"Sure."

Celia looked at the man she loved, and then through the mirror at the boy she cared for as much.

Brian made a good father, strong, but not harsh. Her lips curved at the thought of sharing even more children with him someday. Maybe a little girl who would never dream of running away as she had.

She shook her head then laughed at Brian's inquiring look. First things first. She had to survive this open mic night.

Just one song. The sets were designed for three, but Celia had only one she trusted herself to complete passably.

They arrived just after the night's entertainment started, a fact met with an annoyed look from the organizer when Celia went to the side where she could sign up. She held her case close, and strained to find Nick and Brian in the darkness beyond the stage.

The woman responsible for the performances folded back the curtain and waved Celia past it where she had to wait with the other performers.

Celia's hands started to tremble. So many faces out there, and she'd been unable to see the ones she could trust to love her no matter how lousy she sounded.

"Look honey, they're not expecting much. You do your best, and you'll stun half the audience. The rest will be dazzled by your good looks and won't care if you sound like a dying frog. We get all types here."

Celia turned to smile at the tall redhead scheduled to appear right before she was. "Thanks. Do I really look that bad?"

The woman laughed. "Your hands are shaking so much if your case held bongos you'd drown out the poor guy on stage. Your face is so pale, you're glowing in the shadows." She shook her head. "But don't let any of it bother you. It's all anticipation. Once you step out under those lights, everything else vanishes and you just play."

"What if it doesn't?" Celia hadn't meant to say the words aloud, but they'd come out anyway.

The redhead laughed again. "Well, then, best advice I ever heard was to imagine the audience in their underwear. Trust me, the thought will be so terrifying, whatever's happening up on stage won't hold a candle. And I've seen most of those guys in their underwear, so I should know."

"And now for a set with our favorite doctor, Doc Heather," The announcer called with a flourish, his statement followed by cheers.

"That's me. They'd applaud for anything I did, wanting to stay on my good side." The redhead turned to mount the short flight of stairs even as Celia smothered a laugh, the men and underwear comment taking on a very different meaning.

At the top, Heather glanced back and winked to Celia, mouthing, *You'll do fine.*

Despite the reassurance, the doctor's beautiful voice and easy manner only made the butterflies in Celia's stomach grow stronger. Time flew, and before she had a moment to prepare, the announcer was leaning past the curtain and whispering her name, having apparently announced it more than once.

Celia stumbled up the steps and burst onto the stage only to stand frozen just within the circle of lights.

The announcer caught her arm and guided her to a chair. She sank into it, barely aware of the movement, while the guy talked her up the whole time.

"Celia Baker has not graced our, or any, stage before. Isn't that right? So give her a round of applause to show her we're a nice crowd, won't you?"

He hadn't waited for her to respond to the question, and urged the applause louder with both hands.

"You can do it," came a call out of the darkness in an all too familiar voice.

Melanie.

If she'd been too pale before, Celia knew her skin bore a tarnish of red now, but she found her hands undoing the zipper and drawing out the guitar that had just started to absorb its own energy. This performance would be only one of the experiences etched onto its shiny surface.

Celia ran her fingers across the open strings, making sure Sunsinger hadn't somehow lost her tune in the short car trip to the coffee house, but each note rang true. With no more excuses, she forced herself to look out over the crowd, searching for the one man, one boy, who cared. A family that had claimed her for their own.

When she saw them, her nerves steadied and calm washed over her until she found her smile. Nick knelt on his chair, head propped between his hands. Brian gave her a deep, sensual look that set her insides tingling, and toasted her with his beer.

The doc's advice came to Celia at just the wrong moment.

There sat Brian in his tight shorts without a shred of humor.

Desire flashed through her. A wave of heat raced up her neck to color her cheeks darker, an effect she hoped the others would think caused by the lights blazing down on her.

A cough from the sidelines brought her back to the stage, but Brian's effect lingered. She stroked the strings as if they were his muscles, danced her fingers on the fret board as if playing with his ribs. The words poured from her mouth, a love song just for him. She hadn't written it, but she made each line her own.

She stumbled a few times, missed some notes, and caught her finger on a string, but none of it mattered as she poured her heart out to the one man who made her complete. When the last words trickled from her lips and the last note faded, the audience yelled and cheered just as Doc Heather had promised.

Celia had eyes only for the man who swept through the tables to the stage.

He vaulted onto the platform and hugged her to him, guitar and all, claiming her lips in a deep, nerve-sparking kiss that made the whole world disappear.

At least it did until she heard the applause growing louder and a few wolf whistles joining in. Embarrassed, she ducked her head and fumbled with the guitar case to give herself time to recover.

Brian knelt at her side. "Listen to them, Celia. They want you to play more. You've still got time."

He glanced at the announcer, who nodded his agreement.

Celia shook her head. "That was the only song I had down, Brian. And even so, I made mistakes." A thought crossed her mind, then took hold. "You do it. You take my place. Give them something to remember."

He looked like he would disagree, but something shifted in his expression, something unreadable. "Only if you stay here with me."

As much as she wanted to refuse, uncomfortable with everyone staring, she couldn't take this moment from Brian. She knew, even if he tried to hide it from himself, that staying away from performances ate at him. He no longer had to fear losing his son's affection, or hers. He didn't have to hide.

"I will. Just enjoy this." She moved to stand at one side of the stage, as much out of the way as she could get while keeping her promise.

Brian had a whispered conversation with the announcer, and from the man's expression, she could guess what he'd said.

"Hey folks, we have here for your enjoyment a rare pleasure. Brian Lakes. Living here among us while all the world is searching for him."

Brian glanced at the announcer, confusion on his face, and only then did Celia remember the magazine article and the award, something she'd forgotten in the past few weeks as they spent every waking moment together—and some sleeping ones. He never listened to the radio, and the television was only for movies. He had no way of knowing.

She leaned over to him and whispered, "You're being considered for a Country Music Award."

The grin he gave her made it all worthwhile. He didn't ask for details, didn't demand to know how she'd found out. That would come later. For now, he just lifted her guitar into his arms and stood, balancing one foot on the chair.

Her heart swelled with love for the man she knew, and the one she'd have to come to know. She would never stand between him and his dream, but she would stand at his side. He'd told her what had happened with Kaitlin, and she swore she would never give him the chance to think the same of her. She wanted to share in his love of music, not fight it for him.

Brian leaned toward the mic and waved for silence. "I came here to Foster's Way for peace and quiet. I needed some time to get my life in order." He glanced at her before continuing with a laugh. "What I found was neither very peaceful, nor particularly quiet."

This time he smiled and waved to Nick, who almost fell off his chair in eagerness to wave back.

"But I've never been happier than I am right now. I want to share with you a song I wrote during my time here. I call it *Celia*."

She flushed even hotter and wished for a fan to cool her reddened expression as the crowd roared with approval. But Brian had only to strum Sunsinger's strings once for silence to fall.

Her eyes drifted closed as the words flowed over her, a tale of their unlikely relationship. Laughter rose to her lips and those of the audience as the description of their rocky beginnings unfolded in song, but every word, every note, was infused with a love that swelled to fill the stage, the coffee house, and the world.

No applause came with the last dying note. No noise at all for a long time.

Brian crossed from the mic where he'd been standing and slid the guitar into her case, but when she expected him to pick up the instrument, instead he turned and knelt in front of her.

A spattering of applause started and stopped, sounds of shushing filling the quiet.

Celia stared at Brian, barely aware of the stage or the people beyond it. He'd become her whole focus, but never more so than in this moment.

"I meant what I said up there," Brian told her. "Every word of it. I know we haven't known each other for long, but I want more than just the next week, the next month, or even the next year with you. I want it all, until death do we part. Will you give me that much, Celia? Will you accept all that I am and all that I will be?"

She knelt down and moved into his arms, her lips pressing against his for a moment before she pulled back. "I do...I will. Yes."

He stood up, lifting her with him.

"She said, 'Yes,'" he shouted to the crowd.

On the wave of a roaring cheer, Nick ran to the stage and scrambled up so he could hug both of them as well. "I'm so happy you're going to marry Dad."

Celia bent down and pulled him into a full hug before Brian grabbed hold of both of them.

"I'm glad you're glad," she whispered. "And I'll bet your father's happy you called him 'Dad,' too."

They both turned to see tears running down Brian's face and a smile wider than any they'd ever seen.

"I think they need the stage," Brian said, still grinning. "And maybe we need to go home and celebrate."

Celia shot him an arch glance. "And what would we be celebrating?"

"Why, your stage debut, of course. And your grand entrance into our lives."

Thank You for Reading

I hope you enjoyed seeing Brian and Celia overcome their preconceptions to find love in *Becoming Home*.

If you're willing, I'd appreciate an honest review of *Becoming Home*. Your feedback will help my novel find the right audience.

I like hearing what you think of my stories, so feel free to drop me a line in email to:

* author@margaretmcgaffeyfisk.com

or use the contact form on:

* margaretmcgaffeyfisk.com

And while you are there, if you sign up for my monthly newsletter, I'll share a bit of my writing and publishing journey, fun events, and even snippets or pre-publication stories as a thank you for letting me into your inbox. You can also choose to receive release announcements, which are split into genre and go out only when a new title is available in that genre. Feel free to select as many options as you'd like.

If you'd like to read an excerpt from *Beneath the Mask*, a sweet Regency romance, please turn the page.

EXCERPT

BENEATH THE MASK
Book One of Uncommon Lords and Ladies
(a sweet Regency romance)

In the flash and glitter of the Regency Era, a young noblewoman craves to dance not in the ballroom but on stage, blending music, movement, and soul. Will these scandalous dreams destroy her family, or gain her a loving patron?

So? Which one is it?"

Jasper turned toward his friend and shot Aubrey a heated look. "I think Baker's boy has the best whip hand I've seen for a while. Thatcher, though, can take corners with no regard for the innocent traffic. That alone will shave minutes from his time."

Aubrey jerked the monocle out of Jasper's hand. "You know full well that's not what I'm talking about. Your mother gave you a month to choose a bride, and today's your last day. Who have you chosen?"

Pushing to his feet, Jasper tossed down enough to cover their light lunch, suddenly having lost interest in seeing the end of the cart race. "What does it matter? They're all much the same. Not a single real thought to spare among them. The same teachers, the same dressmakers … they are block prints on the fabric of my life."

Aubrey wisely kept silent as they strode through the streets of London, passing the places frequented by their mothers and heading for those where they'd best not be identified by any of the female persuasion.

Finally, Jasper stopped outside a pub catering mostly to sailors fresh off the naval boats. "I couldn't choose," he said, the irritation clear in his voice. "I couldn't debase myself further by actually considering any of them."

"You're letting your mother choose a wife?" Aubrey asked, horrified. "This is the woman you'll spend the rest of your life with. Can't you find the slightest interest?"

Jasper reached out to clasp his friend's shoulder. "If I do this to please my mother, let her be pleased. If I chose one of them and she turned out to be a hag, I'd have no one to blame but myself."

A surprised laugh burst from Aubrey as he shook his head. "You're an original, Jasper. Never would have thought it out that way, but you're right. She turns out horrible, and you'll be able to wind your mother around your little pinkie. I can see you now, 'I did it all for you, Mother, and see what I'm left with?'"

Pivoting Aubrey so he could push his friend through the door, Jasper grinned. "It's not like I'll see much of her anyway. I'll just whelp a child or two on her and spend my days here in London while she lords over one of my grand properties. We may not have the fancy titles, but my family is loaded."

"A caution, my friend. Your mother's like as not to choose some impoverished earl or duke to bind to the family. I can see her now, going over huge lists to find the candidates who have more title than coin. Oh, and don't forget, those without male line entitlements. If she can't raise her own standing or yours, she'll be sure to raise that of your get. Just imagine when your lady's father passes away and your oldest son outranks you."

Jasper signaled the barkeep. "Two porter, my good man," he called before answering Aubrey. "Does it matter? Her title means nothing once she's my wife. I will have charge of her and all her doings. She'll stay in the country as I will it, and the children with her."

Aubrey looked dubious, but said nothing further as their tankards arrived.

"Just think," Jasper added, laughter gleaming in his eyes, "You're next for the marriage bed. I'm sure your mum could happily find some chit to slip between your sheets."

Choking on his stout, Aubrey glared at Jasper. "I'll do the choosing," he finally gasped out. "I'm not leaving my future to chance as you seem willing to do."

Jasper took a long draw of his beer then wiped the foam from his upper lip. "At least you have a year or two before your mission is proved foolhardy. I tell you, there are no women among that gaggle of girls. Enjoy what time you have of freedom."

The door slammed open and a group of seamen staggered through the entrance, this obviously not the first stop in their day's revelry.

"Come, let's go find a more hospitable location to take our rest." Jasper strolled to the bar to pay his bill, unwilling to keep an account at every place he went like most of his class. The smell of sea salt only brought back memories of what he could have been had either of his brothers survived to sire an heir. He'd been promised the Royal Navy since he wore short pants, but fate had a way of changing things.

"There's a dance troupe not far from here," Aubrey offered. "I've heard they're solid if not exciting."

Jasper forced his mouth to smile. "Solid describes much of my sorry life now. I might as well add another to the mix. It'll give us something to pass the time until we head to White's to check the results and collect my winnings."

Aubrey punched Jasper in the shoulder. "You're so sure of winning?"

"I always do."

A wave of his hand and a hackney pulled up next to them. "Give him the directions, Aubrey, and we'll go see these solid dancers of yours."

"HE'S FROM A GOOD FAMILY with a title even if you'll bring in a stronger one. Lord Pendleton is a baron, not some tradesman buying his way into nobility."

Daphne slipped into the sitting room, wondering how to ask her mother to let her dance. She'd waited for the best moment to raise it, but Monsieur Henre was due back this very day, and she wanted to be able to tell him so. At least they seemed happy now with the question of Grace's marriage resolved.

"And money, dear, don't forget his family properties are exceedingly well managed. The boy goes wherever he likes just so the men can badger him about husbandry and farming. I'll be taking him around our properties myself."

Their mother laughed, gently stroking Grace's arm. "She doesn't care about husbandry, my love. She cares about the husband she'll spend the rest of her life with."

"And titles make the man?" their father asked in a gruff voice.

Rising from the settee, Lady Scarborough wrapped her arm through his. "Of course, dear. Titles are the icing on a delicious snack cake. If you hadn't a title to speak of, my parents would never have let me meet you, much less marry, and see how that turned out."

He patted her on the cheek, his smile so full of love, Daphne almost envied them, but she had more important things to do with her life than marry well.

"Exactly my point, dearest. We have to make sure the boy meets our criteria and then love will come in time."

"He's a man, not a boy," Grace muttered, her gaze modestly entangled with her twisting fingers.

Both parents turned to stare at their eldest daughter, surprise painted on their faces.

"How would you know?" her mother asked.

Grace looked up, her smile a fragile thing to see. "I've seen him at the Mackeley's ball. He didn't seem all that interested in any of us. I wonder that he wants to marry at all."

"Oh posh, no young man wants to be married. They don't understand just how wonderful it is until they experience the bliss themselves. Don't give it a second thought." Mother came to sit next to Grace again, pulling her eldest daughter's hands into her lap. "They see all they'll lose and none of what comes to them. Even my Thomas was reluctant at first, and see what we've become." She sent their father a look.

Daphne felt the tension between them as easily as she'd felt the love. Grace worried them. So much depended on her sister marrying well, but they wanted her to be happy.

Her request no longer seemed favored, so Daphne rose, trying to slip out of the room while they hadn't yet noticed her.

"Daphne?"

She froze as her father called her name.

"I hadn't seen you there. Do you have something to tell us?" Her father tugged out his gold pocket watch and checked the time before looking toward her again.

Daphne squirmed a little, trying to come up with something else she could say instead of begging to be allowed to dance professionally.

Father laughed. "Out with it, my girl. Ask any boon you want on this day. With Grace's future secure, there's little I'd withhold."

She moved to her father's side, pulling him into a hug. "You are the best father in the world," she whispered, meaning every word.

He put his hands on her shoulders and pushed her far enough away so he could meet her gaze. "Now I know something important is dancing around in your little head. Come on and tell your dear father. I never did like to wait on surprises."

Daphne took a deep breath before speaking, dragging her courage about her. "Dancing is right. Monsieur Henre says I'm really good. I'm better than any of his other pupils." The words burst out of her in a rush, then she paused, waiting to see their effect.

Her father mussed her hair and smiled. "As it should be when you do something you love. I'm glad you enjoy dancing so much, but you have to remember there's more to life than just that."

"Not for me." She shook her head. "I want to dance for always." She twirled in a circle, showing them a bit of the routine she'd been practicing.

Catching her outstretched hand, her father moved her through the complicated steps of a line dance until they both sank into chairs, exhausted.

"She definitely gets the dancing from you, Thomas. I've never had quite the balance to pull it off."

Too tired to move, he waved to Mother with a limp hand. "You have grace in other ways that make up for the dancing."

"I had Grace some nineteen years ago. And now I'm planning to let her grow up."

They all laughed at the wordplay as Grace rose to ring the servant's bell for drinks.

Only when they'd sipped lemon tea and nibbled on cucumber sandwiches did Daphne remember her purpose in coming to this room. "Father," she said, catching his attention. "I really am a fine dancer."

He smiled. "I'm sure you are. As your mother said, you come by it honestly."

"I could do so much more than be graceful at my sister's wedding," Daphne said, unsure how to ask.

"Oh, dear." Lady Scarborough put down her cup and rushed across the room. "You don't think we won't take care of you as well, do you? I know it's all been about Grace this season, but you're growing up, too. Don't think we haven't noticed. Once Grace is settled, she and I will give you the best coming out ever seen. Won't we, Grace?"

Her sister nodded, fingers tense around the handle of her teacup. "I'll do whatever I can," she murmured.

"There. You see? Nothing to worry about. You just keep up with your lessons, and we'll find a man worthy of your love as soon as Grace is settled."

Daphne clenched her fists, angry at their preoccupation. "I don't want to marry," she declared. "I want to perform."

The room fell silent. Even Grace seemed stunned by the pronouncement.

Daphne wished the words unsaid, ashamed not of their content but of how she'd offered them. "Monsieur Henre says I'm good enough. He says I'm as good if not better than the dancers in his troupe."

She leapt out of her chair and went down on her knees before her father. "If you would just give your blessing, I could dance for real. I could become famous."

"Get up off the floor," her mother demanded. "More like infamous. What do you think the ton would say if my daughter joined the performers?" The way she said the last word made it sound dirty.

Daphne got up, but only to round on her mother. "They're nothing more than hardworking artists. You wouldn't condemn a poet for living for his art. Why keep me from mine?"

"Daphne Louise, you will respect your mother and honor her word. You are not to make a spectacle of yourself in front of strangers. It's not fitting."

She quailed a bit under her father's firm stare, but tried to stand her ground.

"I had no idea what foolish ideas that Frenchman instilled in her, Thomas. I'll not have him in this house again."

Daphne turned to face her mother, horrified. "You can't," she wailed. "I'll do anything."

Her father took hold of Daphne's shoulders and turned her back to face him. "You're a young woman now. Another year and your mind will be filled with thoughts of a husband and children. I take full responsibility for letting it go this far, but with delaying your coming out for Grace, and your mother being so busy, it seemed a fair exchange at the time. I should have paid more attention when I knew you mastered the formal dances, along with your other studies, long ago." He sighed and shook his head. "It's time to grow up, my dear. To take on adult interests. I know it seems harsh now, but you'll come to understand once you're out in society. Some things are just never done."

She raised trembling fingers to her mouth, water gathering in her eyes as her world tore apart. "I'll never understand," she cried. "Never."

Daphne pulled free of her father's hold and raced through their townhouse until she reached the nursery that had been her home every time they'd come up to London. She threw herself down onto her bed and stared blind-eyed at the ceiling. Never before had she felt so angry, so lost.

Available in eBook, print, and audiobook.
Learn more about *Beneath the Mask*, read a longer excerpt,
or purchase a copy at your
local bookstore or preferred online vendor.

About the Author

Margaret McGaffey Fisk is a storyteller who explores tales across genres and worlds. Raised in the Foreign Service where she developed a love for anthropology, she has been a data entry clerk, veterinary tech, editor, support engineer, and programmer, among other roles. She pulls on her studies and experiences to give depth to the cultures and people that form the heart of her stories. As her website is titled, she offers tales to tide you over.

She'd love to hear from you through any of the contact points or social media accounts listed on her website, or you can subscribe to one of her newsletters for release announcements, snippets, and other news:

margaretmcgaffeyfisk.com/subscribe-to-my-newsletter/

Website:
MargaretMcGaffeyFisk.com

Acknowledgments

While *Becoming Home* is the first contemporary romance I've published, it's not the first I've written nor will it be the last. I started reading Harlequin romances when I was 14, and they became a source of stories where characters put in the effort to make relationships work. This is the spirit I intend to carry forward in my own writing, and so it's appropriate I begin my path into contemporary romance with a book inspired by a Harlequin writing intensive in 2007. The National Novel Writing Month, a challenge I have completed annually since 2003, brought the idea for *Becoming Home* to life as a first draft in the same year.

If you enjoyed this novel, you also have romance author Marie Force to thank because I chose to expand my published romances from historical to contemporary based on information from and support in her writing community.

My husband, Colin Fisk, and my parents and sisters all worked hard to tell me everything I had done wrong, and even what I did right, on the cover art, story, and marketing text to ensure you get to read the polished version rather than my rough draft.

Last but not least, I want to acknowledge your willingness to give my debut on the contemporary romance scene a try. Readers like you make the whole process worthwhile.